# LIVING FREIGHT

**Erratum page 50, line 8 should read:**

"Written by a woman named
Charlotte Bronte..."

# LIVING FREIGHT

## DAYLE CAMPBELL GAETZ

**COVER ART BY
ANTONIO DE THOMASIS**

ROUSSAN
PUBLISHERS INC.
*Specializing in YA and fiction for pre-teens*

THE CANADA COUNCIL | LE CONSEIL DES ARTS
FOR THE ARTS | DU CANADA
SINCE 1957 | DEPUIS 1957

We acknowledge the support of the Canada Council for the Arts
for our publishing program.

We acknowledge the financial support of the Government of Canada through
the Book Publishing Industry Development Program for publishing activities.

The author wishes to thank the British Columbia Arts Council
for supporting the research and writing of this book.

---

## http://www.roussan.ca

Copyright ©1998 by Dayle Campbell Gaetz

National Library of Canada
Bibliothèque nationale du Québec

Canadian Cataloguing in Publication Data
Gaetz, Dayle, 1947-
Living freight

ISBN 1-896184-32-4

I. Title. II. Series

PS8563.A25317L48 1998 jC813'.54 C98-900315-9
PZ7.G34Li 1998

Cover design by Dawn Lemieux
Cover art by Antonio De Thomasis
Interior design by Jean Shepherd

Published simultaneously in Canada and the United States of America
Printed in Canada

1 2 3 4 5 6 7 8 9 AGMV-MRQ 4 3 2 1 0 9 8

# Author's Note

Although this is a work of fiction and most of the characters are creations of my imagination, they are caught up in real circumstances and events of the past.

Many of the characters, such as members of the Douglas family, were people who lived in the time the story is set. I have based the personalities of Amelia and James Douglas, as well as other more minor characters, on their true personalities as much as possible, after reading accounts of their lives. For more information, see "People from British Columbia's Past" (page 165).

The ship *Tynemouth* was the first of many "brideships" that brought young women from England to the colonies of Vancouver Island and British Columbia. The last of them arrived as late as 1920.

*Our most noticeable living freight was an invoice of sixty*
*ladies destined for the colonial and matrimonial market.*

Frederick Whymper, Artist
Passenger aboard the *Tynemouth*

One good thing to come of the cold, Emma reflected as she skirted an oozing pile of sludge that almost completely blocked the sidewalk, it reduces the stink. On warm days the stench of open sewers was enough to make a person choke; and the horrid smell brought on disease, everyone knew that. Trouble is you can't stop breathing just 'cause the air might make you sick, try it and see what happens.

Raindrops crackled all around her, bouncing off the cobblestones, shattering into tiny shards of ice. Emma shivered and walked a little faster, clutching her thin shawl close against her chest. She limped a little more than usual because the cold always worsened the ache in her right hip and knee. In spite of the pain, there was a new lightness to her step. Could be, with the cold weather, her mother's health would improve.

Someone bumped against her on the crowded street, but Emma kept her eyes down, not wanting to be noticed, needing to avoid trouble. Not that she should worry, any *gonoph** who was fool enough to waste his time robbing her—a thin, hungry girl in bare feet, a ragged dress and worn out shawl—ought to start looking for a new line of work.

She had a few pennies hidden deep in her pocket, earned by selling apples on street corners all day, moving about constantly to stay out of sight of the *costermongers*. As she neared the shop, enticing aromas wafted through the door, reminding Emma how hungry she was. She ducked inside. The temporary warmth surrounded her, the smell of fresh-baked bread made her mouth water and her stomach cry out for food. With effort, Emma avoided so much as a glance toward the breadcakes on display in the window.

"Were you able to save me some of the stale bread from yesterday?" she asked the salesclerk.

The stout woman behind the counter had grey hair, a kind face, and tired eyes that wrinkled when she smiled. "No trouble at all, Emma. An' 'ow's yer poor Mam today?"

"'Bout the same, not so good," Emma told her, slipping easily into the idiom of the streets. She pulled a few pence from the pocket of her skirt to pay for the little bundle of hard, dark bread the salesclerk passed over to her. Thanking her, Emma left the shop.

Hunched over her purchase to protect it from the cold, driving rain, black as ink, she at last reached the *nethersken*. Emma held her breath and increased her pace to pass the open cesspool in the court. It smelled bad in

---

* See Glossary on page 171 for explanation of unfamiliar words in *italics*.

spite of the cold and she was glad to reach the stairs.

In the dim, narrow hallway she removed her shawl and shook it vigorously. Dark droplets sprayed from it, spattering walls and floor already black as coal. She stopped at the door to their room and stood for a long moment staring at it. A thought ran through her head, a thought of turning away, of running down the filthy hall, of bursting through the door into the rainy evening. She would run from the city, run until she reached the countryside where clear rain would wash over her and make her clean. The thought was too wonderful to imagine. She was not even certain that rain did in some places fall clear and clean from the sky, or if this were merely a story her mother liked to tell. At the thought of her mother, Emma sighed and swallowed a deep gulp of fear. She opened the door.

The smell of sickness hit her in the face.

"Mam?" she whispered. There was no answer. Emma reached for the candle she always left on the shelf near the door. She tiptoed across the bare wood floor and placed the candle and her small bundle next to a large bowl and a jug of brown water on the old plank they used as a table. Later, she would have to go out and fetch more water from the neighborhood pump, but first she needed to check on her mother.

A tiny window let in little light even in daytime, coated as it was with coal dust. Tonight it was no more than an ugly black square. There was a crooked wooden chair in the closet-sized room, a shelf that held all of their possessions and, on the floor, a straw mattress she and her mother shared. Even so, they considered themselves lucky, at least they had a room to themselves. But for how much longer? Worry pressed hard against her temples. Emma pushed it away.

When the spinning mill was running Emma and her mother both worked sixty hours a week and managed to earn enough to pay the *nethers* and buy bread, potatoes and tea. However, the mill had been shut down now for weeks, because it had run out of cotton—something to do with a war in a place called the United States.

Emma knew they had slaves over there, people with dark skin who were forced to pick cotton. Sometimes, when Emma held the raw cotton in her hands, she felt a strange connection with those poor people so far away. In England the laborers had white skin, but they were slaves to the cotton all the same.

Since the factory closed, Emma and her mother tried to earn their living by buying apples at the market before dawn and peddling them to people on the streets. But the costermongers soon put a stop to that, chased them off their territory. Then her mother took sick and now the few pennies Emma was able to earn went to pay for their meager food. There was nothing left for rent. The one small hope that Emma held in her mind was that the mill owed them some money for the work they had done. She would collect it, if ever the mill opened again.

In the flickering light of the candle Emma could just make out her mother's form—a thin, sunken shape almost lost inside her ragged dress. Emma hesitated again, her stomach sank, she felt ill. She swallowed and forced herself to tiptoe over to the bedside. "Mam?" she said, a little louder this time. Still there was no answer.

Frightened now, she leaned over for a closer look. Her mother lay tightly curled on the mattress, facing the wall, her arms wrapped around one another at the wrists, her long fingers with their painful, swollen knuckles gently rested on either side of her mouth. Her knees were pulled up so that her elbows brushed against the tops of her legs. Her long, brown hair was still twisted into the two braids Emma had done for her last night. The sound of her breath, weak as it was, rattled through her chest. In and out.

Emma bent to pick up the blanket from the floor where it had fallen into a crumpled heap. Some papers fell out, papers filled with scribbled words in her mother's shaky handwriting. Gently she covered her mother's frail body, the thin blanket provided little warmth, but it was all they had. She placed the papers near her mother's hand, knowing Mam would look for them when she woke up. Picking up the pail near the door, Emma set out to fetch some water.

At the pump in the court, she washed her hands and face as best she could and filled her bucket with the brown water. Back in the building, the cellar kitchen was crowded with men warming themselves by the coal stove, tired women preparing sparse meals, and barefoot children running about scrounging for food or simply sitting on a bench and crying. Emma was glad to escape upstairs with her pot of tea.

Her mother had turned over on the bed and her huge, sunken eyes watched Emma come through the door.

"I've made us some nice, hot tea, Mam. You feeling better?"

"Much," said her mother but made no attempt to sit up. She did not even bother to remind Emma to call her Mama, instead of Mam. Her face against the grey blanket was a bluer shade of grey and her skin appeared to be stretched tightly over bone. Her eyes were dark hollows and when she showed her teeth in an attempt at a smile, Emma shuddered. Her mother's face looked so like a skull.

"When I'm gone," began her mother, still not moving, but Emma cut her off, not wanting to hear.

"Let's have our tea," she said and reached for her mother's cup. Hastily she poured the tea.

"No. What must be said, must be said," her mother continued in a surprisingly firm voice. "When I'm gone, you must avoid the workhouse. They'll try to take you away and put you in there where no good will come to you. You'll be kept like an animal in a big, cold ward with nothing more than a cot for yourself. You'll never have enough to eat and they'll make you work all day for your keep. The older girls will teach you terrible habits and you'll never get out again until you run away." Her mother shuddered, as if remembering.

"Mam, you'll get better, I knows it, all you gots to do is try your hardest!" She dropped to her knees and held the white, cracked cup toward her mother.

Her mother grabbed Emma's arm in a fierce grip, slopping some of the tea onto the mattress. "Now don't you start talking like a pauper child. I didn't spend all those years waiting on the Squire's daughters not to learn how to talk proper English. You speak like the gentry and that's the first step to bettering yourself."

And what's so great about the gentry? Emma wanted to ask. She stared down at her mother's thin face, scarcely able to believe Mam still clung to the foolish idea that one day Emma would marry a man rich enough to take her away from a life of drudgery, of working twelve hours a day and getting thrashed if she dared to take a moment's rest. But she could not be cross with her mother, not now, with her so sickly.

"Mama," she whispered, "I don't want you to die."

"It's no good now, Emma, not any more, there's no fight left in me. I hurt so bad. Promise you'll do as I say?"

Emma tried, but could not summon the words, her eyes stung and a painful lump made her throat ache. The sharp bones of her mother's fingers felt as if they would pierce her arm as her mother pushed herself up on one elbow. "Promise me or I'll never rest as long as eternity!"

"I promise," the words were almost inaudible.

"Promise what?" her mother demanded.

"I promise to stay out of the workhouse and to talk proper-like," she grinned.

"Emma!" Her mother tried to sound shocked but her lips turned up in a weak smile as she took the cup of tea.

"I promise to talk properly," Emma said and patted her mother's hand.

"You're getting so like your father was," Mam said wistfully. "So tall and thin. And those dark eyes of yours that look right into a person's soul."

She put down her tea, almost untouched, and leaned back against the wall, exhausted. "I've been remembering him of late, and writing about him too." She fumbled under the blanket until she came up with a sheaf of crumpled papers which she pushed toward Emma along with a small leather pouch, cracked with age. "You must safeguard these papers and one day have someone you trust read them to you. I cannot tell you how important they are, they are my final words to you, words I find myself unable to speak aloud."

He wasted no time. The day after her mother died he came for Emma, a bailiff who called himself Mr. Wiley. He was short, no taller than Emma, with a bulging stomach that pressed so hard against the buttons of his waistcoat that Emma expected them all to come popping off at once. "It's for your own good," he told her as he stood in the doorway, cutting off any hope of escape. "In the workhouse you'll be safe. A young girl like you should not be living on her own, it isn't right."

"I can take care of my own self," she insisted.

He chuckled and shook his head as if she were a foolish child who knew nothing of the world. As if he, a stranger, knew what was best for her. "You'll never earn enough to stay in this place." He looked around at the miserable room, the walls marked with yellow water stains. "You'll end up on the streets, sleeping in doorways or under bridges and you'll soon enough resort to crime—like all the others." He reached his pudgy hand toward her, as if to take her by the arm. "Come now, there's a good girl."

But she had promised.

Emma nodded and turned her back on him. She picked up the blanket from the empty mattress and shook it before folding it carefully, neatly around the candle and the last of the bread. From the shelf she took her old, somewhat crushed bonnet and crammed it on over her dark brown hair that she had earlier formed into braids and twisted about the top of her head. She forced the shoes onto her feet, the shoes her mother had been given by some rich lady who stopped by the street to buy an apple. That must have made her feel saintly, Emma reflected.

There was little else to take. Emma glanced around and her eyes fell upon the cracked white cup—the saucer had long since broken—that her mother always used for her tea. She hesitated, looked over her shoulder at Mr. Wiley, but he was quietly absorbed in a study of his own fingernails. Emma picked up the cup and, pretending to sip, managed to slide one finger inside and slip the ring neatly onto the tip of it.

All the while she refused to think. Since yesterday she had carefully put all her feelings aside as neatly and carefully as she had just folded the blanket. As if she were standing aside, watching herself, Emma could walk and talk and sleep and eat, do all the things required of her, but she did not feel anything, least of all a drop of sorrow. The cup had been her mother's; her mother would never drink from it again. And that was that. She replaced the cup on the shelf.

Yesterday when her mother had twisted the ring over

15

her gnarled finger and given it to Emma, the girl had been horrified. She could not bear to put it on her own finger, so she had slipped it into the cup. Now, today, she needed it. She had nothing else of her mother and Mam had always valued the ring. Emma knew that her father had given it to her mother, long before Emma was born. It had once belonged to his grandmother.

Although she did not dare look at it right now, it was a pretty ring. A wide gold band with an oval of a white, marble-like stone that glittered green and purple and blue when you held it to the light. The stone was set in delicate gold filigree. Emma knew the ring was not worth very much but, even so, she did not trust this Mr. Wiley to see it, for fear he would steal it from her. So she slipped it deep into the pocket of her long cotton dress. The papers were also in there, neatly folded and fitted into the slim leather pouch; those papers her mother had spent so much effort on during her last days.

Emma walked beside Mr. Wiley carrying the bundle that held all of her worldly possessions. The blanket that was now hers alone, a half-used candle, and a crust of bread. She did not dare speak. Not because she was afraid but because with each step away from the home she and her mother had shared, she became more angry. If she opened her mouth now she would tell this man exactly what she thought of him: "I'm not going anywhere with you, you great, fat lout. You dare to tell me what's good for me? Lock me in a workhouse and forget about me? You want to do your good deed and go home to fill your flabby face with meat and potatoes and pudding. You should be ashamed of yourself!"

No, she must not say that. Not if she wished to escape. She must fool him into believing she was willing to go peacefully. The man looked easy enough to fool, the way he strutted along, holding his long nose in the air with his fancy silk handkerchief over it; thinking he's so much better than the rest of us who have nowhere else to live but here. Emma bent her head, ever so slightly, and glanced up at him sideways, as if she had never before laid eyes on a man so splendid as Mr. Wiley.

He stopped suddenly and placed one sweaty hand on her arm, the other hand still holding the handkerchief over his nose. "You seem like a nice enough girl for a pauper, even if you are somewhat crippled."

Crippled? Just because she limped a little when she walked? "And whose fault is that I'd like to know? When you're forced to work in a factory, crawlin' under machines, from the time you're five years old..."

But Mr. Wiley didn't hear. He was too busy looking her up and down in a way that sickened her. "When they get you cleaned up you won't look half-bad either." He squeezed her arm a little more tightly; her stomach shriveled. "I have the feeling you and I will become great friends, Emma."

She did not snatch her arm away but simply stared down at his plump, repulsive fingers until he pulled them away himself.

"You're a strange one," he said, walking a little faster than before, as if he would like to be rid of her as soon as possible. "Do you never smile?"

Emma didn't trouble herself to answer. She had more important things on her mind and her silence made him nervous. She could hear it in his voice. She began to drag her feet so that she trailed slightly behind him. Not much farther now, she would make her move while they were still in her neighborhood and she knew exactly where to go.

Coming up now on her right was a narrow alley, she could see the entrance between two buildings. She glanced at Mr. Wiley's plump back, his short legs as he strutted away. To her horror he stopped, began to turn.

Emma ran for her life.

"Hey!" his voice followed her, loud and angry, it echoed off the brick walls of buildings on both sides of the alley. "Get back here, you ungrateful wretch!"

Mountains of trash were piled in the alley and Emma zigzagged between them, ignoring the pain in her leg. The ground beneath her feet was slippery and foul-smelling, she skirted a dunghill, glad that her heavy cotton dress came down only to her calves, which not only helped to keep it clean but made it possible for her to run more swiftly.

For such a chubby man, Wiley was surprisingly fast. His heavy footsteps pounded close behind her as she darted around a corner to her left. A few steps further and she twisted to the right, into another alley. This entire area was a maze of short, narrow alleyways which were all familiar to her. She turned right again, then left, and, not hearing any footsteps, ducked down three steep stairs to a recessed doorway. Here she crouched, slightly below street level, listening.

Her heart beat fast and hard. She was panting now and the taste of coal dust was thick in her throat. She breathed deeply and the dust seemed to lodge suddenly in her lungs, choking her. She would rather die, right here and now, than cough. She tried to collect some moisture in her mouth, dry with the bitter taste of coal that hung in the air. She swallowed, gagging with the need to cough. She listened for footsteps and heard none. Still she refused to cough, though her eyes felt as if they would burst from their sockets.

Hours later Emma still had not moved, even though her cramped position made the pain in her hip almost unbearable. One moment she told herself that Mr. Wiley must have given up by now, he must have gone home, or bustled off to drag some other poor soul to the workhouse. The next minute she was certain she recognized his footstep, strutting along the alley above her head. What if he were waiting for her, knowing she must return sooner or later to the main street?

And so she remained crouched into a ball, clutching her knees against her chest, afraid to look up until darkness fell thick around her. At last, so stiff and cold that she was barely able to stand and drag her aching legs up the stairs, she emerged from her hiding place. She did not retrace her steps but took a long, twisting route back to the main street. Then, under cover of darkness, she walked determinedly away from her old neighborhood with no idea of where she was going or where she might sleep that night.

The rain began again, straight black needles through the thick air, cold as ice. People scurried here and there, each with their head down, each with a purpose, somewhere to go. Emma walked on alone, huddled over her folded blanket which she held tightly pressed against her stomach in an attempt to keep it dry. She was tired now, limping badly, and shivering with the damp and cold. The night stretched in front of her like the long, cold street; dark and hemmed in by thick mist. Emma had never been to this part of the city before and so did not know the places to hide, the safe havens from the rain. Her feet dragged in her ill-fitting shoes as she walked on and on, wanting with every step to rest but knowing too well the danger of stopping, perhaps falling asleep, being caught off guard.

She paused in front of a two-storey brick house, a *toffken*, she thought, trying to picture the people who lived there with their fancy clothes and even fancier manners. The house was set back about ten feet from the street behind a low brick wall. An ornate wrought-iron fence ran along the top of the wall and made the overall structure about four feet high. A wrought-iron gate, leading to a cobblestone court in front of the house, stood slightly open, inviting. On the right side of the house was a large bay window that jutted out over the court. To the left was a white wooden door with a brick pillar on each side and a narrow roof above, just enough to protect the doorstep from the rain.

All this she saw in the dim light of a street lamp almost a half block away. The neighborhood seemed quiet enough, the house looked respectable and clean. She would rest for a few minutes out of the rain, perhaps it would stop before she was forced to move on. She squeezed sideways through the gate, not touching it in case it creaked, and crept slowly toward the door, listening all the while. Everything was quiet.

Emma stepped under the small shelter above the door and squeezed up against the inside of a brick pillar, out of sight of the street. She unfolded her blanket enough to retrieve the candle which she stuffed into her pocket and the crust of bread which she stuffed into her mouth. The blanket she wrapped tightly around her shoulders. Even though the bread was tough and difficult to chew, Emma ate every crumb and could have eaten three times as much.

With her back against the pillar, she closed her eyes and tried to think. What would become of her? She had no family now. All she knew of her father was that his name had been Joseph and he died in the big typhus epidemic back in 1848, months before Emma was born. Her mother told her that if he had not died, they would have remained in the country, perhaps to have started a farm of their own. They certainly would not have moved to the filthy, overcrowded city of Manchester.

Emma had no friends she could turn to either, there was no time for friends when you worked all week and your mother expected you to go to school on Sundays, your one day off. She snorted. That was another of her mother's foolish fantasies, wanting Emma to learn how to read. What good had reading ever done anyone? Her mother could read and where did it get her? Nothing but an early grave. In those few hours a week, Emma had not learned much, she was always so tired. All she really wanted to do on Sundays was sleep.

She was exhausted now too, and wanted only to sink to the ground, curl up into a tight ball and sleep the night away. But no. Someone was sure to see her. If she were to survive this night she had to remain alert. First thing in the morning she would buy some bread with the few pence she had left in her pocket. Beyond tomorrow she would not allow her mind to travel.

Emma's eyes shot open, she had all but fallen asleep. She glanced quickly around. What was that sound? A footstep? Where did it come from? She turned her head to one side and listened more carefully. Another footstep, several heavy steps made by more than one person. Voices accompanied the footsteps, men's loud drinking voices, and then a burst of ugly laughter that made her stomach recoil in fear. She could see them now, in silhouette, two bulky figures at the gate, the first one pushing it open wider.

"The boy forget to close your gate again, Jack?" said the other.

"Mmm, either that or I've got a visitor."

Emma's heart raced, she had to get out of here before they reached the door or she would be trapped. Quietly she raised the blanket from her shoulders to cover her head, the dark grey would help her blend into the shadows. She slipped around the pillar, keeping her head bent, careful not to make a sound. The men stopped to latch the gate, not ten feet away from her, "You can't be too careful these days," one of them said, "with the crime rate the way it is."

"Disgusting," said the other. "These people think they've got a right to take our hard-earned money while they sit back and don't do a thing to help themselves."

"The poor need to know their place," the second man agreed.

Emma ducked down low and, dragging her right leg behind because the joints had stiffened while she rested, she sneaked under the overhang of the bay window. The deep shadow should be enough to shield her.

"Do you see that?" one of the men yelled. "Look, under the window, someone's there!"

She had reached the far end of the window by then and straightened up running, forcing her leg to work. Darting around the corner of the house she found herself in a narrow lane, less than three feet wide, that stretched into darkness.

"Hey! Get back here, you!"

Footsteps clambered after her, but Emma was sure she could outrun them, fat as they were, if only the lane did not end, if only she was not trapped. Already she could hear them puffing, the gap between her and them widened, she ran into almost total blackness, with one hand in front of her, feeling the way, the other clutching her blanket.

Her foot clattered against something, probably a dustbin, the sound rose into the night and echoed off the brick walls above her head. She stumbled forward, her weight shifted to her right leg which gave out under her, sending her crashing to the ground. She pushed herself up and continued on, more slowly now, feeling her way.

To her right she sensed more than saw a narrow opening, felt a slight movement of air against her face. She reached toward it with one hand. The footsteps were close behind her now. She ducked inside, pressed herself up against a damp brick wall and stopped breathing.

The footsteps were muffled by the coughing, sputtering and panting for breath of the two overweight men.

"I don't like it," one of them said, his voice high-pitched, nervous.

"She can't be far away," the other gasped, coughed, and then added, "I'll catch her and wring her dirty little neck."

"Could be she's leading us into a trap. Could be there are others of her kind out there just waiting to rob us."

"Nonsense," said the other. There was a long, tense silence. "We'll teach the little blighter a lesson," he added uncertainly.

"Did you never hear of a *bearer-up*?" At that precise moment a rough shout echoed between the buildings, not so far away. It was followed by the sound of scuffling feet.

"I say we go fetch a *Bobby*," said the first voice.

Emma smiled as the two scuttled back the way they had come. She said a silent thank you for the well-timed shout. After waiting for as long as she dared, Emma stepped from her hiding place and walked out of the lane.

Back on the street she splashed quickly over the wet pavement, her thin shoes spraying grimy water onto her dress. After about a block she slowed to a brisk walk, not looking this way or that, she must not call attention to herself.

The pain in her hip lessened as she forced the joint to work and she concentrated on disguising her limp. The rain had stopped but in its place a solid dampness hung thickly in the air, clogging her eyes and nose with its sickly smell. She paid little attention to where she was going and so was surprised when her surroundings gradually began to look familiar. Less than a block away a gas lamp glowed dimly through the darkness and fog. And then she recognized the entrance to the factory.

Of course! A perfect place to take shelter for the night. With the factory shut down, no one would come around here, she would be safe. She hurried up the steps to a small covered area, closed in on three sides, in front of the entrance. Exhausted, she shrank into the darkest corner, pulled the blanket tightly around herself, and sank to the ground with her knees bent almost to her chin and her back against the corner post.

The night was still black when she awoke to a scraping sound. Emma felt no momentary confusion as to where she was—like a young, wild animal she was instantly alert, instantly on guard. She tried to make herself smaller, quietly pulled the blanket more closely about her face. All her joints ached now after her long, cold sleep. She heard the jangle of keys, words muttered under the breath, a key slide into a lock, the door creak open. When the door slammed shut again, Emma sat up straight. Did this mean the factory had opened again?

She removed the blanket and attempted to smooth her hair. Then she stood up and brushed at the heavy cotton of her skirt, as if she could clean it by doing so. Good thing it was a nice dark color that would not show the dirt.

She waited to see if other workers would arrive. When they did, Emma walked in with them.

The master, Mr. Smith, recognized her and pulled her out of the line. His thick eyebrows raised up high on his bearded face as he looked down at Emma. "Wot you doin' 'ere?" he demanded.

"What do you mean? I work here."

The part of his face above the dark beard turned bright red. "Now listen up. We been open two days an' you 'aven't bothered ter show yer face. Wot do you think this is? Charity? I warned you before, you lazy child, either do yer work or someone takes yer place."

"But…me mam died, I…"

Far from inspiring any spark of humanity, her words made him even more angry. He stepped closer to her, until his pink, slobbering mouth was inches from her face. "There you go," he bellowed, "as if shirkin' yer work in't bad enough—talkin' back to a master, now that's grounds for instant dismissal!"

She stepped back to avoid the spittle that sprayed from his mouth. "You owe me money," she said, struggling to keep her voice even, "a week's wages I never got before you shut down—and me mam's wages too."

He stood stock still and glared down at her, as if she had committed an unpardonable sin. "You want charity—go to the workhouse!"

Emma refused to back away as she might have done just a few days earlier. Now she was on her own in the world and she was desperate. Her empty stomach reminded her that she needed this money if she were to eat for the next few days. Beyond that she refused to think.

She took a deep breath, squared her shoulders, and looked him in the eye. "We, both of us, earned it," she said firmly. "We worked hard and now you owe me our pay."

Gradually Emma became aware of a strange sound in the room around her. Not strange so much as unusual, and not really a sound either. It was more like—silence. She glanced about. No one was working. Everyone was watching her. And she felt suddenly afraid, certain that every one of them was hostile to her, that they wanted her to leave, to go quietly away, not create a fuss, each one afraid for her own job.

"Give the girl her money," said Margaret, the woman who had worked close to Emma's mother for years.

Emma's head jerked around in surprise.

"God knows she earned it," said another, "and her mother too. Paid with her life, she did."

"Yer oughter be ashamed, firing the child and her mother just gone to her grave, where's yer sense o' decency, man?" This was Margaret.

Mr. Smith narrowed his eyes and looked from one end of the huge room to the other, his face was growing redder by the second. Emma was not sure if this was because the room was so hot and stuffy or because he was so angry. "Get back to work right now, or I'll fire the lot o' you!"

"Can't fire us all," Margaret pointed out calmly. "Then where'd yer be?"

Emma stood absolutely still, trembling a little on the inside, unable to believe what was happening. She watched Mr. Smith's face turn from angry to worried as he thought over Margaret's words. It would take days to hire new people, days more to train them all. The owners would demand to know why the factory was not producing right now, taking advantage of an unexpected shipment of raw cotton. "I can start with you," he said and smiled triumphantly at Margaret.

There was a quiet roar in the room. Everybody in the factory, from those long rows of machines, moved forward as one to crowd close around Smith. For a long moment there was complete silence. Mr. Smith did not move a muscle, his mouth was a pink circle in his dark beard, his eyes traveled from one determined face to the next. Then with an angry sweep of his arm he turned to Emma, "Go to the bookkeeper, take the note I give you, an' ee'll give you the money."

A collective sigh went through the room, an easing of tension, as most of the workers returned to their chores.

Mr. Smith handed her a hastily scribbled note. "When yer done get out o' my sight," he bellowed, "if I ever lay eyes on you again I'll..." he raised his right hand as if to strike her, but paused and glanced about the room. The tension closed in around him, as thick as the fog on the streets of Manchester. It seemed to Emma that Mr. Smith shrank before her eyes from a big, fierce bully with the power to terrify her, into a small, middle-aged man with a bald spot on top of his head and a heart blacker than the coal that fired the machinery. Slowly he lowered his hand. "Go," he said weakly.

Emma's step was light as she turned away. Many of these people she had barely spoken to in all the time she had worked in the factory and yet every one of them had stood behind her, against Mr. Smith. She smiled a thank you to Margaret and then, as she moved down the long aisle, nodded gratefully to the workers on each side of her. The air in the room seemed almost festive.

Hunched over, facing into a bitter wind, Emma shuffled along the dirty street. The weak sun that filtered down between the buildings held no warmth for Emma, with her clothing still damp from last night's rain. She bought some bread and a special treat for herself: fresh cheese. The storekeeper gave her a generous slice and wrapped it with the bread in a piece of blue cotton. Emma settled on a low wall to eat her breakfast and tried to form some sort of plan.

"They gots to let you stay in overnight, that's the law," said a man's voice nearby.

Without moving her head, Emma swung her eyes in that direction until she could see the speaker out of the corner of her eye. Two men dressed in dirty, tattered clothing had stopped to talk.

"Aye, but they don't like it, afraid of us overnighters, they are. Think we're out to rob the place," the other man replied.

His companion laughed, "As if there'd be summut worth stealing in a workhouse!"

"Makes no matter to me. I gots enough money together, workin' as a *navvy*, it'll buy me passage."

There was a long pause before the other man spoke. "Where yer 'eaded then?"

"An' you 'aven't 'eard? Young Queen gots 'erself a new colony four years since. British Columbia, they calls it— fancy sounding name if I ever 'eard one. Go there and you picks up gold withouts 'ardly looking fer it. Gets rich in no time, guar-an-teed."

The other man laughed. "Go on! Yer been listenin' ter too many stories."

"I tell yer I'll be a rich man come this time next year. See if I'm not."

The other man laughed again, "I'll see yer in the workhouse like as not." He slapped his friend on the back before the two walked off in opposite directions.

"British Columbia," Emma repeated under her breath, she liked the way it sounded on her tongue and repeated it several more times so she would not forget. She pictured the country in her mind, a land that sparkled with gold wherever the sun shone upon it.

Gradually the large, smelly factories gave way to smaller, more attractive buildings. Before long she came to clean streets lined with rows of two-storey houses, each with its own short flight of stairs. Women moved along the streets, chatting, wearing such strangely beautiful gowns and bonnets they made Emma want to slink past with her eyes averted, hoping not to be noticed. But she could not keep her eyes off the dresses, they were so narrow at the waists and then suddenly stuck out so far that by the time they touched the ground they formed an enormous circle around the women's feet. How on earth did they manage to walk in such dresses, with their legs lost somewhere in the middle of all that material? The skirts were like bells and their legs the clappers.

Emma glanced up at the doors to their houses and wondered how they ever managed to squeeze themselves through. Did they have to tip their skirts up sideways in order to get inside? She imagined one of the ladies falling over and almost laughed aloud at the thought. Surely the poor woman would have no choice but to lie helplessly on the ground, waving her legs frantically in the air until she was at last rescued by two strong men and set on her feet again.

Here came two young ladies toward her now, with a sour-faced older woman trailing close behind. The first young lady was dressed in beautiful blue, soft as the sky and shimmering with a light of its own; its shifting colors changed with every movement. Emma had no idea what the material was, she only knew that it was not cotton. Her fingers itched to touch it, to feel its cool smoothness under her fingertips. The young lady wore a warm cape and a bonnet with blue ribbon on it to match her dress. The other young lady, who was forced to walk a step behind because their dresses took up so much space on the sidewalk, was dressed similarly to the first, but in green. It was like nothing Emma had seen before—a deep, dark beautiful emerald green.

Emma could scarcely believe such loveliness existed. Knowing she should look away, she could not keep herself from staring. The young lady in blue had a perfect complexion: milky-white skin and cheeks touched with a hint of pink. Her cold blue eyes turned on Emma and made her wither inside, ashamed of her dirty, ragged cotton dress, her crumpled bonnet, and her unwashed face. She dropped her eyes, as though she had no right to occupy space on the same earth as such a person. Even so, she could not resist a glance sideways at the other, the lady in green, as they passed one another. She was astonished to realize this young lady could not be much older than herself. Her eyes matched the green of her dress and they regarded Emma, not with hatred or fear but with curiosity, even friendliness. She smiled and her green eyes sparkled.

Caught by surprise, Emma took a few seconds to return the smile. When she did, the older woman charged forward to hustle the girls away as if they were in some sort of terrible danger. Her face, turning to Emma, was so contorted with hatred that Emma gasped and stepped sideways.

"Stay away from our young ladies, do you hear?" she said. "Imagine, the likes of you, wanderin' streets where you don't belong, pesterin' yer betters with yer filthy ways. Next thing we know you'll be knockin' at the door, beggin' for food! Well, all I can say is, we don't need the likes of you around here and the sooner you clear out the better!"

Emma's cheeks burned as she hurried off, head bent. She was aware of passing other people but did not look up, not once; she could not bear to see the expression in their eyes, whether it be pity or anger.

When at last Emma left the city behind, she slowed down and gazed about in wonder. Never had she dreamed the world could be so beautiful. From the track where she walked, the moors rolled gently into the distance, all soft browns and gentle greens, ending where a row of jagged peaks thrust up through mist that floated in wispy veils on their lower reaches.

Spotting a tree that stood alone in a field of short grass, Emma wandered off the track for a closer look. She had learned about trees on the Sundays she spent in school, she had even seen drawings of them, but in those drawings the solid, brown trunk always disappeared up into a huge ball of green leaves. This one had no green leaves, no leaves at all, and the sight of it made her sad. She reached out and touched the trunk, felt its roughness under her fingertips. Above her head the trunk divided into branches which spread outward, splitting again and again into smaller and smaller sizes until each one finally ended in a thousand twigs that curled up and out to meet the darkening sky. So still. So silent.

For some reason that Emma did not fully understand, she was reminded of the church she and her mother had often visited on Sunday evenings in the last few weeks before Mam took sick. Thoughts of her mother began to creep into her consciousness, threatening to overwhelm her, but she immediately pushed them aside, as one might push away an unwanted object; shove it into a closet and firmly close the door, forget it ever existed.

The ground beneath the tree was covered with a thick blanket of brown leaves, the top layer as dry and crisp as paper. Emma shuffled her foot, digging into the leaves. Underneath was a mushy, wet mass, slippery but not foul-smelling, not like the smells in the city. The scent that rose up from the leaves lingered pleasantly in her nostrils; earthy, comforting, welcoming.

She was tired now, and hungry. The short day was almost over, twilight would soon descend into darkness.

Emma decided to go no farther. She spread out her blanket and settled herself close to the trunk of the tree, out of sight of the track. She pulled the top half of the blanket tightly around her shoulders as some small protection against the cold, and opened her package of bread and cheese.

For the next three days, Emma spent every minute of the few daylight hours walking. She still had no idea of where she was going but was happy to leave Manchester farther and farther behind. When she ran out of food she bought more at a village and later at a farmhouse, but her money was disappearing at an alarming rate. Wherever she went she asked if there was any work to be done but always received the same reply: those who are looking for work go to the city, not away from it. There is no extra work on a farm, especially for a girl, and certainly not at this time of year.

And so she trudged on.

Somewhere, in the back of her mind, Emma knew she should be worried, but she wasn't, not yet. In a few days she might very well be starving but there was nothing she could do about it right now, so she would not think about it. She had never known such freedom in her life before, and she almost believed she could go on forever. Her eyes followed the track that stretched on ahead of her, over the next hill, around the next bend. She could hardly wait to get there; could scarcely imagine what exciting things she might discover.

Each night felt colder and seemed to last longer than the one before it as she lay curled up and shivering in her thin blanket under a hawthorn tree or nestled out of sight of the track in a quiet wood. Her joints ached with the cold, especially her right hip and knee, but the days were pleasant enough once the sun melted the early morning frost. By noon its weak rays reached out to touch Emma's cold skin as she walked along the track and by early afternoon she was comfortably warm, a warmth that lasted until the shadows began to lengthen. With twilight a chill crept out of the damp ground, a chill that grew steadily deeper as the night progressed.

On the morning of the fifth day when Emma sat up, hugging her arms against her chest for warmth, she was surprised to see that there was not a touch of frost on the nearby grass. She looked up through the dark stubby branches of a hawthorn to a sky that hung grey and gloomy over the tops of the surrounding trees. Hungry, Emma reached for the package of food she had tucked inside her blanket the night before. It wasn't there.

Puzzled, she glanced around, first close by and then, standing up, farther afield. There, not far off, caught in a clump of brown grass, was a hint of blue cotton. She ran over, picked it up. It was her parcel all right—or what was left of it. The cloth had been ripped to shreds and there was no sign of the breakfast she had so carefully set aside from last night's meal. Absently rubbing a fragment of blue cotton between her fingers, Emma wondered what small animal was sleeping right now, content, with a full belly, thanks to her.

She raised her fist, clutching the strip of cloth. "Do yer see me stealing the food from yer mouth? Do yer see me chasing after yer very own mice an' rabbits an' eatin' 'em? Not on yer life! An' I'll thank yer to keep yer grubby little paws off my food in future."

So saying, she turned and continued along the road, for the first time strongly aware of her mother's presence. It loomed over her and around her, crying out in silent disapproval. Emma realized she had lapsed into the way of talking she had heard all around her as she grew up, a way of speaking her mother would never allow.

Her mother, who had worked in a house that belonged to the landed gentry, had carefully studied and copied their manner of speaking. According to Mam, the way a person spoke was the most important consideration if ever you hoped to better yourself, and so she made certain Emma learned to "talk like the gentry."

Now, walking along this lonely track, Emma wondered again why her mother had left a comfortable job as house-maid in a good home to move to the dirty, overcrowded city. Every time Emma had tried to ask her, Mam refused to discuss it. As she walked, to keep her mind off her growing hunger, Emma tried to imagine what it would be like to have a real bed, a bed of your very own to sleep in every night. How would it feel to fall asleep with never any hunger pangs clawing at your insides? To wake up in the morning and know that in spite of a long day's work ahead of you, at least you would be warm and have enough to eat? If such a life were really possible, why would anyone be such a fool as to walk away and leave it behind?

Lost in her thoughts, Emma did not at first notice the sizzle of raindrops spitting into the dry earth of the track. When they became stronger, she lifted her face to greet them: cool they were, and clean, just as her mother had said. She closed her eyes and let the soft rain wash over her face.

Hours later the rain had turned to a downpour and Emma shuffled along the deserted track in her soggy shoes, with her head down, soaked through to the skin, and so hungry her stomach ached. The sky closed in around her, gloomy and grey, as though she were all alone in the world, a feeling heightened by the fact she had not seen so much as a sign of another human being all day.

Rounding a wide bend she came to a sudden stop. A small whitewashed farmhouse nestled snugly against the hillside, its thatched roof blending in naturally with the background. A curl of smoke drifted from the stone chimney.

To Emma the house meant warmth and food. She felt in her pocket for the little money she had left and hurried toward the farmhouse. Excited, filled with sudden hope, she raised her cold, wet fist and knocked on the wooden door. Moments later a woman opened it, just enough to let the rich smell of fresh-baked bread spill out around her.

The woman was in her twenties, short and plump with dull brown hair gathered at the nape of her neck, from which long strands had escaped and fell across her face. She wore a white apron over a plain cotton skirt. In one arm she held a small child, with the other hand she rubbed the creases on her forehead as if they hurt. Dark circles around her eyes did not hide the wariness in them as she first caught sight of Emma.

Along with the smell of bread, the sound of children's voices also tumbled out the half open door as the woman studied Emma. She looked from the top of the soggy, straw bonnet that Emma was certain must be sitting crookedly on her head to the heavy cotton skirt that clung limply to her legs. Hours ago Emma had given up trying to keep her blanket dry and wrapped it around her shoulders in an attempt to get warm, but, as she stood cold and dripping on the threshold of this farmhouse, leaning toward its warmth, smelling its good food, she shivered uncontrollably.

"Please," she said, "could you spare me a crust of bread? I'm hungry and I have little money left."

The woman stepped back, blocking the door, closing it to less than six inches. "Get away with you. D'yer think I'm after givin' food ter every *moucher* wot comes ter me door? The nerve of yer! Yer thinks my children should go 'ungry just so's yer can fill yer belly? And yer never doing a day's 'onest work in yer life. Why yer no more 'an a worthless *skipper* by the looks o' yer."

"If I'm a skipper it's because I have no place of my own to sleep. And I don't choose to be a moucher, I would work if there were work for me. Maybe you know where I can find some? Could I help with your children for the price of a meal?"

The young woman looked terrified at the thought. "Get away with you before I calls my 'usband on yer. Go back ter the city where yer belongs." And without another word, she slammed the door in Emma's face.

Disheartened, Emma dragged on up the track, her feet heavy now and hurting with every step in her tight, wet shoes. The only good thing was that the rain slowed down and gradually came to a stop. Soon after, a weak sun broke through a thin layer of cloud.

Late that same day she came to a village. As she passed through Emma watched the people move about in their dry clothes, people who looked as though they never lacked for food. She wondered if they realized how lucky they were. It was good to know that everyone's lives were not as miserable and hopeless as that of a poor factory worker in the city. These country people had clean air to breathe and clean water to drink. They might work hard but at least there was something to look forward to in each day. Emma made up her mind right then and there, she would rather die than return to work in the city. Somehow she would find a way to live in the country, to work on a farm the way her mother had always wanted.

However, she had more immediate decisions to make at the moment. She had only a few pence left to her name and had not eaten a thing all day. And yet she could not bring herself to ask for help, could not bear to see that look come over people's faces, the glazing of the eyes, the sign that told her she was unworthy of associating with their kind, not good enough to be a part of village life. She was no more than a moucher, as the woman at the farm-house had said.

She walked on, keeping her head bent, her eyes on the ground, avoiding curious, accusing eyes, wanting only to get through the village and be alone. She passed a shop that smelled of bread and could not resist a sideways glance. There, in the window, were cakes of bread, rows and rows of loaves. Emma could almost taste them. Her mouth watered and her stomach cried out. She hurried on.

The ringing of a bell made her stop. Halfway up the low hill that led out of the village she saw the short, square spire of a church. When she reached it she stopped again. Next to the church was a small, neat house surrounded by a soggy garden of neatly clipped evergreen shrubs and empty, muddy flowerbeds. All was surrounded by a low hedge. A narrow stone pathway led up to a white door.

Should she go in? Would she be turned away? She chewed on her lip and did not move. Her mother had insisted a church was one place that should be open to all. Men of God, she said, pledged to help others—whether rich or poor, innocent or sinful—even if some of them forgot that promise.

Emma hesitated, shivering and hungry at the end of the path, afraid of rejection. If she were turned away here, what would be left for her?

No. She could not face it. She started up the street. After about ten steps she slowed down. If she continued on, out of the village, what then? What would become of her?

Emma turned around and walked boldly up the path to the white door.

The door swung open and a huge woman loomed in the doorway. Tall and imposing, somewhere in her fifties, she was neatly but plainly dressed. Wrinkles fanned out from the corners of her eyes and her dark hair was streaked with grey. She folded her arms across her sagging chest and glared down at Emma.

The girl cringed; she suddenly felt very small and getting smaller by the second—as if she were shrinking down and down into a pair of shoes that were growing bigger, stretching to swallow her up. Her mouth dropped open but no words came out. Too late, she wished she had continued on walking, anything would be better than this final, brutal humiliation—to be branded a moucher, to be sent away with a stern warning never to return.

And then the big woman smiled, the wrinkles around her eyes deepened, became friendly.

Emma stopped shrinking. Her knees went weak. Such a

kind face, a square, solid face that contained no hint of accusation, not a whisper of superiority. Emma could even dare to hope this woman would not chase her away with no more thought than if she were a stray animal.

Even so she could think of nothing to say. Almost afraid of breaking a spell, she worried that if she should speak even a few short words, the woman would suddenly come to her senses, would realize that Emma was nothing more than a desperate pauper, a homeless skipper, not worthy of effort, certainly not to be trusted.

"Come, child," the woman reached a large, square-fingered hand toward Emma and stepped back to invite the bedraggled girl inside. "You're soaked through and half frozen, you'll catch your death of cold out there! I shouldn't wonder if you're half-starved as well."

Tentatively Emma stepped inside. She was rewarded by a sudden rush of warmth. In front of her a coal fire burned in a friendly sitting room and she longed to go closer. The woman looked Emma up and down, "Aye, and we don't have clothes to fit you, little bit of a thing that you are—if our Annie were at home—but then she's gone off and married hasn't she?" the woman bustled down the hall, "Well, we'll just have to make do with an old dress of my own."

An hour later Emma sat at a hand carved wooden table in front of the fire, devouring a bowl of soup. It was more delicious than anything she had tasted in her life before. Also, she was exquisitely warm and cleaner than she could ever remember being. The woman, who said her name was Mrs. Barnes, had insisted that the housemaid fill up a tin tub with hot water from the stove. At first Emma had eyed it nervously. She could scarcely believe that she was expected to remove all her clothing and actually sit in the water. But Mrs. Barnes was not a woman you could say no to easily.

It had not been half-bad, she reflected now, once she got used to it, the warm water sloshed around her, soaking off layers of dirt. And now, sitting here lost in a dress that could have easily included two more of her, she realized that she felt much better for having had a bath, not nearly so itchy. She didn't smell half-bad either. She put her hand tenderly against her chest and felt the little hard lump. Her mother's ring. Emma had found a length of wool and slipped the ring onto it, then tied the wool securely around her neck under the dress.

The housemaid was busy carrying out pail after pail of dirty water from the tub and not too happy about it either, judging by the grumbling noises she made each time she passed by. Mrs. Barnes was seated in an armchair near the window, fiercely studying a piece of needlepoint that she held in both hands. Suddenly she flung it onto the table beside her chair. It slipped and tumbled to the floor. "It's enough to drive you insane!" she shouted.

A spoonful of soup stopped on the way to Emma's mouth, her eyes darted toward the large woman and away, searching out the assistance of the housemaid who was just disappearing from the room, carrying another pail of bath water, muttering to herself. Insane? Was that the explanation? Alone, trapped in a house with a very large insane lady and wearing her very large dress. She really should be going—oh, but she was so hungry!

She would just finish the soup, then leave. Emma raised the spoon, took in the soup—meaty and rich, filled with vegetables and beef—she swallowed, stared down at the thick, hot liquid, the potatoes and carrots floating in it. If only it weren't quite so hot, she could eat it a whole lot faster. She filled the spoon again, lifted it from the bowl.

"Boredom!" Mrs. Barnes bellowed.

Emma jumped, her hand shook, liquid spilled over the edges of the spoon, her eyes shifted until she could see Mrs. Barnes from the waist down.

"It drives you insane faster than anything! And this," she bent over, picked up her needlepoint, "I go cross-eyed simply looking at it!"

Emma tried to think. Was she expected to say something now? Her eyes sought out the big woman's face and quickly darted away. Mrs. Barnes was leaning forward on her chair, glaring at Emma as if to demand an answer.

"My mother's eyes hurt too," Emma blurted out, "so she was happy when the law said women and children had only to work a twelve-hour day."

When Mrs. Barnes made no reply Emma turned toward her. The woman was sitting very straight, her eyes wide, her mouth slightly open; she could not have looked more horrified if Emma had pulled out a knife and threatened to rob her. Emma's heart contracted suddenly and painfully. This woman would surely send her away now that she realized Emma was not the person she expected,

46

whoever that might be. Carefully Emma ate what was left on the spoon, put the spoon down, closed her eyes, and tried to gather strength for the angry words to come.

"My dear girl," said Mrs. Barnes, "you must think me the most ungrateful soul ever to have lived. There you are, near to starving with no home to go to and not clothes enough to keep you warm and you come here only to listen to my complaints!" When she paused, Emma opened her eyes. Mrs. Barnes was leaning forward again, staring with an intensity that took Emma's breath away.

"You must understand that I want so much to *do* something! If I could, I would help all the children like you who toil their lives away with never food enough or a decent place to sleep."

She leaped to her feet. Emma stared up at her, afraid to blink, wondering again if the woman had taken leave of her senses. Or, could it be that she had none to take leave of?

"No!" Mrs. Barnes shouted. She seemed to take up the entire room, waving her arms about. Emma bit her lip. "The men only laugh in their condescending way and tell me to, 'Behave like a lady, don't worry your head with business.' As if I didn't have a brain in my skull." She picked up the needlepoint, stared at it with distaste, and tossed it angrily across the room. "Where's the purpose in this, I ask you?"

"I-I'm sorry," said Emma, trying to understand.

Mrs. Barnes hesitated. "Oh, and now I've frightened you with all my noise and carrying on," she said in a surprisingly soft voice, "just trust me to do that." She sat down heavily. "Come on then, eat your soup. When you've finished you can tell me all about yourself, and we'll see what's to be done."

The sound of muffled voices woke her. She opened her eyes but was afraid to move because she was so high off the floor and the bed was so narrow. The tiny bedroom was shadowy and dark, lit only by a faint glow of moonlight on the small square window. She turned over carefully, nervous of falling, and began to sink back into sleep.

"Emma," she heard Mrs. Barnes say quite distinctly, although her voice was muted by distance. She also caught the words "hungry" and "alone."

A man's voice answered, not so loud as Mrs. Barnes, a muttering from somewhere below. So, Mr. Barnes, the *choker*—no, she must not use that word—the parson had come home. Emma was a half-step from sleep when the word "workhouse" leaped up at her, straight through the floor, spoken in the man's voice. Her eyes flew open and in one motion she pushed aside the bedclothes and swung her feet to the bare wood floor. But softly. She put her feet down softly and raised herself off the bed. Taking pains not to make a sound she padded toward the door.

With the door open a crack, she could see a faint flicker of candlelight from below. She squeezed into the passage. Now she could hear the voices, clear as though she were in the same room.

"We can't take in every beggar child that comes knocking at our door, surely you realize that Amanda, my dear."

"And how many children have we taken in? It's seldom enough a poor creature finds their way to our door and when they do I feed them, clothe them as best I can, send them on their way, and shudder to think what becomes of them. Does no one care? I would take every one of them in if only I had the means. I would feed them and teach them all how to read and write."

"The poor have their place, just the same as any of us. God made us what we are and it's not for us to change it."

"Nonsense! If it's not for men of the church to change such injustice, then who will? God didn't make the poor, the factory owners made them and want to keep them that way, so's they have more for themselves."

"Can you never try to understand, wife? They're not like you and me. Give them too much food and a little idle time and they'll sink to the depths of debauchery, sure as I'm sitting before you. Believe me, we're doing them a favor by not indulging them. Besides we have the work-house for those that can't care for themselves."

There was that word again. Emma shuddered. She would have to run away soon, this very night. But, oh! She was so tired.

"She'll not go to the workhouse. The girl promised her mother on her deathbed that she would never go there, and I'll not let it happen. Emma will stay with us until we find something for her."

The parson muttered some unintelligible words.

"Have you seen the inside of a workhouse?" his wife demanded.

There was a long pause. Then, quietly: "Yes. You're

49

right. I cannot in good conscience send anyone to such a place. Especially so young a girl."

A chair creaked and a shadow fell across the candlelight. Emma hurried back into the bedroom and closed the door softly.

Mrs. Barnes closed the book she had been reading aloud. Emma was fascinated by the story, she had no idea books could be so interesting. Written by a woman named Emily Bronte, it was called *Jane Eyre*, and in the chapter they had just been reading, Jane was wandering about the country-side, cold and hungry and alone, just as Emma had been.

"I wish I could read like you do," Emma said wistfully.

"But you can read some, you have the basics." Mrs. Barnes held up the thick book, "I wouldn't expect you to read a book such as this one, not yet at least. Your mother was right though, to send you to Sunday School: learning to read is most important if you ever hope to better your-self." She reached over and patted Emma's hand. "Don't you worry, you're doing just fine. A little more practice, and you'll be reading as well as anyone." She pushed a sheet of paper toward Emma and began to twist the top off a bottle of ink. "Now, let's see how your handwriting is coming along."

Emma dreaded this lesson. Clutching that thin little instrument between her finger and thumb, trying to make the tiny lines and loops Mrs. Barnes expected of her, and worst of all, trying not to leave those ugly blotches of ink on the paper, seemed next to impossible. She was certain her hands were too big and clumsy ever to do a good job of it and yet Mrs. Barnes, for all her great size, had lovely handwriting. The worst thing was, and this she could not bring herself to admit, the lines and loops made no sense at all to her, they looked nothing like the letters in books.

Emma bent over her task, seated at the small desk near the window, so absorbed that the tip of her pink tongue peeked out through her lips. The last three weeks had been good to her. With wholesome food, rest, fresh air and a clean place to sleep at night, she had filled out slightly, her cheeks were pink and her dark eyes bright. Even her hair, always a dull, stringy brown, now shone with a luster of its own. Often when she passed the mirror that hung over the fireplace, Emma paused to stare in wonder, unable to believe the reflection looking back was really her own.

Outside now, the afternoon sun sank low in the sky and the light grew dim where Emma worked. A damp wind blew through the leafless trees in the garden. Emma tried hard to copy the sample set for her. Mrs. Barnes had been so good to her, Emma wanted to please her. But this handwriting business was so very difficult!

As she worked, she wondered to herself what would become of her. She dreaded asking, afraid of what the answer might be. Last night she had again overheard Mrs. Barnes talking with her husband, they had kept their voices low and Emma had only been able to pick out a few words here and there, but the name "Miss Angela Coutts" had stood out, along with "steamer" and "Vancouver Island." She had no idea what any of this meant but hoped it had nothing to do with the workhouse.

Mrs. Barnes settled on her rocking chair with a book open on her lap. Emma glanced at her. She wanted to ask if they were about to send her away but could not force the words past her lips. She opened her mouth, cleared her throat, and closed it again. Maybe she was better off not knowing. This way she could dare to hope Mrs. Barnes would let her stay; she could be so happy here.

The days grew longer, buds appeared on the naked trees, flowers filled the garden with their color and perfume. Like a small child just learning about the world, Emma delighted in every change. She helped Mrs. Barnes prepare the soil and plant peas and parsnips and potatoes in the kitchen garden behind the parsonage. When the first tiny shoots poked out of the ground she almost danced with excitement.

She worked hard in the garden, weeding around the tiny plants, later planting the less hardy summer vegetables. She loved the feel of sunshine on her shoulders, enjoyed knowing she was a real help to Mrs. Barnes.

On an early evening in mid-May Emma was hunkered down between two rows of peas, admiring the young healthy plants when Mrs. Barnes called her into the sitting room. She ran inside, eager to tell Mrs. Barnes which plants had just come up, which ones were already in bloom and which ones were being attacked by insects. "Wait 'til you see," she began and stopped. Mrs. Barnes had a glum look on her face. Mr. Barnes sat across from his wife looking uncomfortable.

Emma stood awkwardly in the center of the room, wearing a neat and simple dress of printed cotton that Mrs. Barnes had made for her. Emma thought it luxurious and it fit her perfectly. She was a tall girl and her tough life had made her strong. With her rest from strenuous work, the ache in her hip was barely noticeable and the limp had all but disappeared. In the last month her figure had filled out and her dark, flashing eyes made her face interesting, if not beautiful.

She glanced at the parson, sitting back with his chubby fingers clasped over his round little belly, his high collar pressing against his neck. A choker, she thought and a smile flashed behind her eyes.

He seemed to pick up on this and his little eyes bored into her face. Emma held her chin up and tried not to show how he made her feel. The time had come. The parson had won. She was to be sent away. What a fool she was to have thought otherwise, to have let herself grow fond of Mrs. Barnes. Even before the parson opened his mouth Emma made up her mind to run away as soon as possible, that very night, if he so much as mentioned the workhouse.

"I must admit she looks almost tolerable, now that you've had all these weeks to work on her."

"Tolerable! Why, she's a lovely girl, quite as lovely as our Annie. And she can read and write too, at least as well as can be expected under the circumstances."

"I won't have you comparing her with our daughter," the parson said sharply, sitting up abruptly. "It won't do. What are you thinking of, wife?"

Emma looked from one to the other, wondering why she was here. Neither of them spoke a word to her, but they discussed her as if she were not present. Mrs. Barnes did not answer her husband, even Emma knew there was no point. He had already worked himself into one of his angry moods. The man could not tolerate anyone contradicting a word he said, and it made not a jot of difference whether he was right or wrong.

He raised his hands to the height of his shoulders and slapped them down impatiently on his thighs. "Give the child my decision then," he said, as if it were beneath him to speak to Emma himself and he wished to get this unpleasantness over with as soon as possible.

It was all Emma could do to keep from blurting out: "What's to become of me?" But she held her tongue and did not say a word.

"There is a woman who lives in London, named Miss Angela Burdett-Coutts," Mrs. Barnes explained, choosing her words carefully. "Now, Miss Coutts has a great deal of money, all of her own, and she devotes her life to doing good work, helping the poor wherever she is able. It seems that she has heard of the many young men who live in one of our newest British colonies. Most of these men are without wives. Women are needed to help settle the land, to create a peaceable, Christian colony in the name of Great Britain.

"Miss Coutts, having heard of this problem and also

having visited workhouses where she sees dozens of young women who face bleak futures, has decided to solve both problems together. She has agreed to pay passage to the colony for many of these destitute young women. Upon arriving, they will be taken on as servants or governesses to the few families living there. Unless, of course, some of them should happen to meet and marry with certain of the bachelors soon after arrival.

Emma listened politely, wondering what any of this had to do with her. Then the parson spoke. "I have made all the arrangements. You are to be one of those young women. The ship sails from Dartmouth in a fortnight. As Mrs. Barnes has planned a visit to our daughter in Bristol, she will accompany you and see that you arrive safely before the ship is to sail."

Emma pressed her face against the cold, hard glass of the porthole. She needed to see for herself exactly what would become of Elizabeth. Something scuttled over her foot. She shuddered but did not look down, it was too dark to see her feet anyway. Instead she kicked out sideways, missed, and heard the rat scurry off to join its hungry companions.

Now the coffin appeared; small and cheaply made, it was hoisted off the ship by four strong sailors. Emma shivered and wrapped her arms more tightly about her thin body. The weather had turned cold again as they plowed steadily south toward Cape Horn. It was August now, but, strangely, that meant winter down here in the southern half of the world. The cold, following the heat of the tropics, had been more than Elizabeth's delicate health could endure. Like most of the girls, she had never in her life eaten a proper diet or lived in a comfortable home, and such a life can make a person old before they ever reach twenty years of age.

Watching, Emma shed no tears. Crying accomplished nothing and she had no sympathy for those who wasted their energy in such foolish self-indulgence. Night after night, as girls all around her cried themselves to sleep, Emma forced her thoughts away from this terrible prison of a ship. She must not break down; must not fall apart; must remain strong. She had kept her promise to her mother, the only thing that really mattered. Just once had she come close to tears, the night she learned Mrs. Barnes did not want her; that she was sending her on some terrifying voyage to the other side of the world. There was no future for her in England, Mrs. Barnes insisted, in the New World she would have endless opportunities. But Emma knew the truth. Mrs. Barnes simply wanted to be rid of her.

The coffin was almost out of sight now, merging into the bustle of activity on the dock. Perhaps Elizabeth was the lucky one. She really had escaped; she could never again be locked below decks, as Emma and the others were. Emma would miss her though. Of the sixty young women, Elizabeth was the only one who had befriended her when she arrived on board, lonely and confused after saying goodbye to Mrs. Barnes. Up until that very last moment, she had dared to hope Mrs. Barnes would change her mind, would ask her to stay with them.

Now Elizabeth was gone too.

A sudden, powerful image came to Emma. The image of Elizabeth, or of her spirit at least, floating over the harbor, above the trees, becoming a part of every particle of air, every droplet of water. Emma closed her mind to it. Dying might be one way of being set free, but it was not the only way and not the best way either. Dying meant giving up, it meant no second chances. Emma meant to improve her life, not give up on it.

"Goodbye Elizabeth Buchanan," she whispered, "God bless."

"May you rest in peace," added Mary, who was standing at the next porthole. "Lord knows, the rest of us won't."

Emma glanced at Mary. The two of them, both befriended by Elizabeth, had become closer during Elizabeth's final days. Mary was at least two years older than Emma but not so tall. She had straight, dark hair and a frightened look in her eyes whenever you caught her unaware. Mary refused to speak a word of her life before boarding the ship and Emma did not press. Sometimes, however, she wondered at the deep sadness she glimpsed in Mary; a sadness the older girl took pains to hide under a mask of humor.

Emma and the other girls, those who were well enough, had begged the Reverend Scott and Mrs. Robb to allow them ashore on the island. Or, failing that, at least to allow them above deck, to smell the salty air, to rid their lungs of the stench of their fetid cabins where they had been imprisoned since leaving Dartmouth. But the two chaperones refused.

*Chaperones,* she thought, jailors is more like it. She would remember and curse those two for as long as she lived: the high and mighty Reverend William Scott, a man

58

with not one sympathetic bone in his body; and Mrs. James Robb who held herself to be so far above the girls that she managed to turn a blind eye to their suffering. Neither they nor their families were locked up day after day, and yet the two took it upon themselves to guard the girls against any "lascivious attentions" from the crew. This also applied, it seemed, to every man on the Falkland Islands as long as the steamer was docked here at Port Stanley to take on fuel and make repairs.

For her part, Emma would gladly suffer a little lascivious attention in order to escape for a few moments from this cabin, which in her mind was worse than the workhouse she had managed to avoid. At least the workhouse did not creak in the wind, did not sway back and forth, up and down on sickening waves. Even more importantly, the inmates of a workhouse were permitted to step outside for at least a part of the day.

Only once had Emma come close to escaping. One night she and Elizabeth had managed to work open the cabin door and creep up the companionway toward the deck. Excited, filled with anticipation of open air, bright stars, and a cool breeze, they could not stop themselves from laughing. But the hatch was locked against them. It would not open no matter how frantically they pushed at it. Defeated, they returned to the cabin, or cell, as Elizabeth called it, so disappointed neither of them could speak. Emma was convinced that experience marked the beginning of Elizabeth's illness.

She turned away from the porthole and Mary, determined to put Elizabeth from her mind just as she had earlier put her mother from her mind. She needed no one. If ever you let yourself care about people they either died or sent you away. Emma wondered what life in this new land would be like. What if it were worse than her life in Manchester? Was such a thing possible? She stifled the little clutch of fear that grabbed at her, just slightly below her rib cage, threatening to take hold.

"Vancouver Island," she whispered. It had a good, strong sound to it. She wondered if it was very far from that other colony she had heard of, "British Columbia," the land that glittered with gold.

She knew of course, they all knew, the real reason the girls were being sent. The colony lacked young, marriageable women. Emma didn't feel very marriageable. She certainly did not look forward to marriage to a stranger in a wild land—a man who might very well be as cruel as any of the powerful men in England. Besides, she never wanted to depend on anyone else. And so she hoped to find employment. In her more optimistic moments, she even dared believe she might be taken in as a housemaid in the home of some kind family, as her mother had been. The difference would be that she would stay in the job, at least until she found a way to British Columbia and the gold that waited for her there.

Emma sank onto her bunk. Enough of such foolish dreams. Her task for the next several weeks was simply to stay alive. Every day she walked, back and forth, back and forth, in the tiny cabin, exercising her joints so she would not be lame when they arrived at their destination. Nevertheless, with the poor food, the cramped and damp quarters, she knew her leg was getting worse.

"There's nothin' 'ere," Mary commented sadly. The two of them pressed their noses to a salt-encrusted porthole for their first look at Esquimalt Harbor in the early morning of September 18, 1862. Although the *Tynemouth* had steamed into the harbor late the previous evening, they had been unable to see anything in the dark.

"Yes there is," Emma replied. "Look over there, on that point. See that row of buildings? Look how clean and neat they are, and they all have gardens in front of them. And look down there at the end of the cove. You can see some buildings through the trees. It looks like a farm. And here, see the size of that house? Someone rich lives there, I'll bet. How would you like to work there? I certainly would, and then there are some buildings that look like a hospital and…"

Mary reached over and placed a hand on Emma's forehead. "I'm thinkin' the girl's got the fever, chatterin' on like she's gone altogether del-er-i-ous, she is."

"Well, but I'm just so glad to be here, Mary, I don't think I could stand another day on this ship. And I do want to get a good job, don't you?"

Mary regarded her with a kind of pity. "Of course, we all do." Then almost as an afterthought, added, "Just don't get your 'opes up, that's all."

"We'll be getting off this ship soon, that's all that matters right now. Besides, this isn't Victoria, it's only Esquimalt—a place for ships to dock and nothing more."

"An odd name for an odd place," stated Mary.

The harbor was filled with boats of all descriptions, from ocean-going steamers, to large navy sailing ships, to gunboats, to long, narrow boats cut out of single logs and paddled by local Indian people.

"Esquimalt is the new British naval base for the Pacific," Emma informed Mary, having recently overheard this news from Mrs. Robb.

"All right then." Mary pulled her shoulders back, stuck her nose in the air and perfectly imitated Mrs. Robb's voice: "If you behave like a pwoper lie-dy, you may be lucky enough to mawwy youwself a sie-lor."

"Now wouldn't that be just lovely," Emma grinned. "He would be at sea most of the time and I would have some freedom for once in my life."

"How poifect," Mary continued, still imitating Mrs. Robb, "and you will be so busy taking caaw of all youw blessed little babies that you will not have a moment's time to behave in an impwoper manner."

"Well, I never!" said Emma, throwing a hand against her chest and pretending to look shocked. "As if any of us would behave in a manner unbefitting to a lady. Why, there's not a one of us that doesn't admire Mrs. Robb and aspire to be as kind and generous a lady as she herself is."

Both of the girls laughed.


For almost 100 days now they had been prisoners aboard this dreadful ship with nothing to do and no fresh air to breathe. Those days had dragged slowly into one another and somehow passed, Emma had no desire to look back at them and, even if she did, would be hard pressed to distinguish one from another. But now, finally, they had reached their destination. They could look out the porthole and see the land that held their futures. To be cooped up now was torment. But cooped up they were, for what reason no one seemed to know.

Emma looked out at the wild and empty land. Beyond the buildings clustered near shore was nothing but trees. Hills rose gently toward the sky, covered in dark green forest. No big buildings, no ugly factories spewing their black smoke into the air, no crowds of people. She liked the untamed, clean look to it; the look of new beginnings. Her Mam, who hated being confined, who longed for fresh country air and the open moors, would have loved this land. She would have stretched out her arms to embrace it.

The ship remained anchored in the harbor. All the passengers had disembarked, all except the sixty girls in third class. Emma thought she would go mad with the need to get outside. Even so, every so often a little knot of fear clenched at her middle when she thought of stepping ashore, into the unknown. Then she would remind herself that nothing could be worse than this endless waiting, watching the world out there, so close, and yet not being a part of it.

A visit from a local newspaperman was the highlight of the two days. He strutted among the girls, looking them up and down over his fat mustache, as if he were inspecting a herd of horses about to be led to market. He stopped in front of Mary. "May I ask how old you are?" he asked.

"You may—so long as yer don't 'spect an answer."

"What's your name, then?"

"It's Mary, wot's yours?"

"Amor de Cosmos," he said, raising his nose another notch and hooking his thumbs under the lapels of his jacket.

"Wot kind o' name is that, then?"

He glared down at her and started to walk on. Then, turning slightly he said, "It's a name I gave to myself and it means that I'm a man who loves the entire universe."

As he strolled away Mary whispered to Emma, "Looks to me like that one thinks he *is* the entire universe."

"As a matter of course, we went aboard the steamer yesterday morning and had a good look at the lady passengers. They are mostly cleanly, well-built, pretty looking young women—ages varying from fourteen to an uncertain figure; a few are young widows who have seen better days. Most appear to have been well raised and generally they seem a superior lot to the women usually met with on emigrant vessels."

Amor de Cosmos
*The Daily British Colonist*

At last the moment came. A key clicked in the lock, the door opened, and Emma struggled up the companionway behind the others, filled with excitement and fear. Even before she stepped out on deck a blinding pain slammed into her eyes, forcing them shut. She stopped. The bright light glinting across the water made it impossible for her to see. Three months in the dark and now I've gone blind, she thought and placed both hands over her eyes. She forced them open just a slit, enough to peek between her fingers and see that the other girls were suffering too.

Then she noticed the air. She had never smelled anything so wonderful! She took a deep breath. The taste of it lingered in her throat, fresh and clean and salty.

Through her fingers she squinted at a gull gliding over-head on a brisk wind, it cried out and another gull answered from somewhere in the distance. The bird's white underside and outspread wings made a pure white cross against the deep blue of the sky. But Emma's eyes ached, she closed them and stood completely still, letting the cool breeze wash over her face while she thought about that gull, free to let the wind blow it where it pleased. When she was rich, she would be like that gull…

"Huwwy along thewe giwl! What's the matter with you?" Mrs. Robb spoke harshly and Emma opened her eyes enough to see that the girls were being herded aboard a smaller vessel. She followed.

A man with long legs and sideburns that met beneath his chin greeted them on deck. "Welcome to the gunboat *Forward*. I'm Commander Lascelles, and I promise you a pleasant, if brief, voyage to Victoria."

They were ferried across the choppy water, around a long point of land and into Victoria Harbor. Emma's eyes watered annoyingly in the wind and sun but she managed to open them wide enough to catch her first glimpse of her new home: a haphazard collection of wood huts creeping down over solid rocks that dropped steeply to the water's edge. Narrow wooden stairways ran right down to the water itself where small boats bobbed gently at anchor.

"Wemember to keep yow eyes lowuued and walk modestly," Mrs. Robb reminded each of them as they disembarked, "pewhaps you will be lucky enough to be selected."

Mary and Emma exchanged glances. They both knew what "selected" meant and from the looks of the men they had seen so far, neither of them wanted any part of it.

The September day was warm as they climbed awkwardly into smaller boats, carrying whatever belongings they might possess. The bright sun made seeing difficult, and the fact that they had not exercised for three months made them clumsy. A noisy crowd of onlookers shouting lewd comments from shore did not help either.

As Emma climbed down to a rowboat, a young sailor, noticing her difficulty, reached out a hand to help, but Emma ignored it and settled into the boat on her own. On the way to shore she reached over the side and trailed her hand in the water. It was cold and so clear that looking down she could see golden brown seaweed waving in the current on the rocks below. She pressed the cool water against her eyes to soothe them.

Mary touched her arm and nodded toward shore. They could see the crowd more clearly now. Most of them had full beards and hair that covered their ears under the brims of their hats. They wore jackets and vests and breeches of various cuts, most of them black or dark brown. Every one of the men was watching the rowboats as if their lives depended upon them. As her boat neared the dock, Emma felt suddenly afraid. She pressed her lips together to keep them from trembling. She refused to look at the men or listen to their thoughtless words.

For a moment she wished she were back on board the *Tynemouth* where it was safe and nothing was expected of her except silence. Climbing clumsily onto the dock, she noticed several buckets of soapy water lined up in a row, and for a hopeful moment wondered if perhaps the men were not gathered to ogle the girls at all, but were simply here waiting to scrub down the dock once everyone had passed by.

Mrs. Robb was waiting for them, her arms folded across her chest. She started talking and although Emma did not choose to listen, the words penetrated her consciousness anyway. "Giwls, just look how thoughtful the good citizens of Victoiia awe. They've pwovided you a means to clean youa extra clothing—if you have any—befowe entewing the town."

On her knees, with every move as she scrubbed her spare dress and underclothes Mrs. Barnes had given her, Emma's anger grew. What was the meaning of this indignity? Whose idea was it? Surely this washing could wait until they reached the privacy of their quarters. She glanced at the girl to one side of her. Julia was a tiny child, frail, with milky white skin and pale red hair. Emma saw her set face, the tight angle of her jaw and knew the effort she was making to fight back tears. Less than a month before the *Tynemouth* sailed, Julia had been snatched from her widowed mother who could no longer manage to feed her. Julia was only twelve years old.

On her other side was Jane. Jane was one of the older women who had paid her own way to Vancouver Island. She had saved for years for this chance to improve her life. Trained as a teacher, she looked forward to being self-sufficient here in the colony. Emma looked at her face, blotched and purple with anger, and heard her muttering to herself while she scrubbed the clothes so hard Emma thought she would wear them right down to rags, if she didn't swing around and fling them at someone first.

The men tried to outdo one another with their rudeness and with each obscene comment an eruption of coarse laughter spread through the crowd. Some tried to break their way through, like wild animals, but were held back by police and marine officers. Emma wondered what her mother would think if she could witness what was happening; she wondered what Mrs. Barnes would think of the place she forced her to go; she was glad Elizabeth did not have to endure this. Her eyes stung with unshed tears, she swallowed against the lump in her throat. Then she lifted her head high and stared disdainfully at the men. She would never let them win.

The worst was yet to come. With the washing done the young women were lined up, two by two, and paraded through the town just as if they were a shipment of livestock to be looked over before purchase. On each side of the dusty streets were dirty, roughly dressed men, shoving each other, vying for attention, and shouting horrid words that hurt right through to her soul. Emma had never seen anything quite so revolting and was glad she had arranged to walk beside Julia. She glanced at the small girl and saw a tear trickle down her pale cheek. Emma reached over and held Julia's arm to reassure her.

"We'll be all right," she whispered, "once we get to our quarters, just you wait and see."

Julia nodded and bit her lip. She swallowed, but could not speak. Her eyes held such a look of helplessness and fear that Emma knew she was a long way from being comforted. But what comfort could there be?

Nevertheless Emma continued to hold Julia's arm and both did their best to ignore the men. Julia stared at the ground while Emma glanced around, taking everything in: the saloons that far outnumbered every other type of business; the rows of attached brick buildings, at the front of which were brick columns joined to one another by gracefully curving arches. On the second storeys, rows of arched windows continued the theme. This part of the city reminded Emma of the glimpses of San Francisco she had caught from her porthole when the *Tynemouth* had slipped through the Golden Gates and stopped in the bay for fuel.

The next street was lined with wooden buildings of varying sizes and shapes, and in front of them, planked sidewalks sheltered by roofs that were supported by upright beams.

"Watch you don't call attention to yourself or you'll be snatched up before you know it," Mary whispered from behind.

But Emma refused to keep her head down, her eyes fixed on the dusty streets. She wanted to see everything; she wanted to breathe deeply, to enjoy the freedom she had so longed for during the past three months. She refused to let these repulsive men spoil it for her. "No one would dare snatch me," she replied fiercely.

Even as she spoke a man stepped out of the crowd and started toward her with a lopsided grin that twisted his lips sideways. A short, muscular man, he had obviously washed his face and hands just before coming here because his neck was the color of coal and contrasted sharply with the white circle of his face. He looked her up and down, avoiding her eyes, and then smiled in a glazed sort of way that made her wonder if he was ill.

Emma was a tall broad-shouldered girl, and she pulled herself up now to her full height. She glared into the man's face, narrowing her eyes in a warning to leave her alone. At last his gaze reached her face, met her eyes, and a look of shocked surprise came over him. He stepped back uncertainly. Hearing the jeers of the men behind him he stepped forward again and grabbed the arm of Anne, the girl in front of Emma.

"Marry me," he said. "I like the looks o' you."

Anne hesitated for only a moment. She glanced at the frightening crowd lining the street and back at the nervous young women she was walking with; she looked at the man and seemed to conclude that he could offer some sort of protection. "All right I will," she answered uncertainly.

Emma glanced over her shoulder at Mary, who shook from head to toe with a terrible rage. Suddenly Emma's own anger evaporated and was replaced with something far worse: an empty, aching sadness. Whether the sadness was for Anne, for little Julia who looked to have shrunk inside herself with fear, or for herself, she could not have said. Perhaps it was for all of them. In spite of everything that had happened to her, Emma had an idea that a marriage between two people, two people who would have to spend the rest of their lives together, should be decided on something more than the jeering of men and a grab on the arm.

She glanced over the crowd again. That's when she noticed him—a young man standing back from the others, staring straight ahead as though he were embarrassed at the behavior of his fellow men. He looked like a big, overgrown boy but was strongly built, as though he worked very hard. His clothes were rough cut but clean enough and his light brown hair curled just slightly, beneath his wide-brimmed hat. His eyes met hers and he smiled. Before she could stop herself Emma smiled back, then looked quickly away.

"I saw that!" whispered Mary, "I warn you, you'll be snatched up before you know wot 'it you."

"Not me," Emma insisted but she glanced again toward the young man and carefully hid her disappointment when she saw that he had gone.


"How shall I choose? They're all so weak and scrawny, I don't expect any one of them could do a decent day's work," said a middle-aged woman with a well-fed look about her. She wore a large hat pulled down low on her brow. Her enormous skirt encased her body like one of the tents at the edge of town. Attached to large hoops, it swayed from side to side like a ringing bell as she walked.

Emma watched her, fascinated. She wondered how the woman had managed to pop herself through the narrow doorway leading into the marine barracks. She glanced at Mary who raised her eyebrows and grinned, ever so slightly. Emma choked. She pressed her hand against her lips to hide the laugh that lurked just beneath the surface.

The woman's eyes flicked toward her, cold blue under sagging eyebrows, her thin lips turned permanently downward. Emma looked quickly away, studied the ground near her feet. She could not afford to antagonize this woman. She must at least give the impression that she "knew her place." Already she had discovered that here in Victoria, just as in England, there was a sharp division of classes. Those who owned property considered themselves "upper class" and looked down on working people and servants as if they were a different breed, as if they were put on this earth only to serve the needs of their "betters."

In only a week many of the girls had already found positions as servants. Anne married that miner from Sooke who grabbed her by the arm and hastily proposed. No one had seen her since. And Julia had gone too. She and another girl had been whisked off to a place called New Westminster, which sounded quite grand but most probably was not, to work for a woman named Mrs. Moody who had five children to care for. Emma hoped Julia would be all right. In some ways she envied the younger girl, not just because she had found a position, but because New Westminster was across the strait in British Columbia, the land of gold.

Emma's first priority was to find a job. She shuddered at the thought of the men who constantly lurked around the barracks, hoping to snag themselves a wife. If she did not get a job soon, she might be forced to marry one of them, either that or starve to death. She had yet to make up her mind which would be worse.

Feeling the woman's eyes still upon her, Emma looked

up and smiled in what she hoped was a quiet, respectful manner. But the woman turned to Mary. "This one will do," she said, "provided I may return her if not satisfactory."

After Mary was led away, Emma noticed another woman, quite different in appearance. Her clothes were simple and practical. Her skirt hung almost straight down, without hoops or petticoats, and stopped several inches above the floor. She wore no hat and her dark hair was pulled back severely at the nape of her neck. Her amiable brown eyes and broad face appealed to Emma.

Emma smiled and the woman returned the smile. She walked over. "I need a girl to help me in the kitchen," she said, "now that my older daughters have married. My husband does a lot of entertaining. Do you think you would like such a job?"

Emma was about to say yes when Mrs. Robb came bustling over with a determined expression on her face. "Mrs. Douglas!" she shouted, "you don't want that giwl, I have one over hewe who is much moue obedient and not lame either."

Mrs. Douglas? Wife of the Governor of both Vancouver Island and British Columbia? Surely she would not want her, a tall scrawny girl with a mind of her own, one who occasionally let people know exactly what she thought.

"This girl suits me," Mrs. Douglas said firmly and turned away from Mrs. Robb. "What is your name?"


As they walked the short distance to the Douglas home,

Mrs. Douglas reached into the pocket of her skirt, pulled out something red and shiny and round, and offered it to Emma. Emma hesitated. An apple. Although she had sold apples on the streets of Manchester, she had never dared bite into one. The cost would be too great.

"It's an apple from Nisqually. I think you'll like it. Go on, taste it."

Emma licked her lips, holding the apple, looking from it to Mrs. Douglas. Mrs. Douglas nodded encouragement. Emma took a bite. The apple crunched between her teeth and the crisp, clean flavor burst into her mouth. She could not believe anything could taste so good. She swallowed and felt its goodness trickle down to her chest, to her stomach, through her entire body.

"Thank you," she said, and took another bite.

Tall Joe bent close over his work in the failing light. By now it was almost impossible to detect a hint of color. His knees hurt from kneeling on the gravel bar. His eyes ached from staring into clumps of sand and gravel, one after another, sloshing about with water from the creek. One more time. Holding the shallow, flat-bottomed pan in both hands he turned it in continuous circles, allowing the water to spill over the steeply sloped sides. Sand and grit slopped out with the water, leaving the heavier pieces behind. Joe tipped the pan to catch the light of a pale moon which was just now rising above the ragged gap between evergreens high above the streambed. The weak light just caught a faint glimmer of gold.

Tall Joe grunted and picked out the tiny pieces, placing them carefully, one at a time, in the leather pouch he always kept in his pocket. He was tired. A full day's work, from dawn to dusk and, if he was lucky, he had made enough to cover food and supplies. At times like this he wished he had stayed home. Or, better yet, he wished he had not squandered those first riches, the ones that came so easily to him down in California back in '49.

Thirteen years, he reflected as he pushed himself tiredly to his feet, gritting his teeth at the pain that rammed through his knees as if a spike were being driven into the center of each kneecap. Thirteen years, he thought again when he was safely standing, and only once had he struck it rich. The money that had come so easily back then was long gone now, every penny of it.

Joe, in his mid-thirties, was still a good-looking man. His unusually tall, lean frame gave the impression of suppressed power. His thick, brown hair stuck out below a wide-brimmed hat, curled over the collar of his cotton shirt, and mingled with the unkempt beard that had sprouted during the long, arduous weeks spent on the trail. Tall Joe was not a man to give up easily, he had come to this land to make his fortune and refused to return home without it, no matter how long he took.

It seemed there was nothing to return home for anyhow, his lovely Jenny had not waited for him, despite her promises. She refused to answer any of his letters, even in the beginning, even when, for a short time, he was rich enough to send for her. He often wondered what she did with the money he sent for her passage. Probably used it as a dowry when she married; he felt his cheeks flush with anger as they always did when he thought of Jenny marrying someone else.

Not that he could honestly blame her. Jenny was so beautiful, with her shining brown hair, her sparkling gold eyes and a smile that could melt a man's heart. She had a voice like beautiful music, it made him happy simply to listen to her.

Of course he knew about Thomas Brooke, the gentleman farmer Jenny's father wanted her to marry, in spite of his age. The man had been in love with Jenny for years. The pressure from the two of them must have been too much for her to bear.

Joe knew his Jenny would not have given that Thomas Brooke fellow a second thought as long as he, Joe, had been there. But he had been young and sure of himself and had left her behind to run off and seek his fortune. He had promised to come back for her inside of two years. Even better than that he had sent for her within a year. But she never came.

No. She had up and married Thomas Brooke just as soon as he left, sure as anything. Women are like that, always looking out for themselves. And yet, once in a while, just lately, he got a terrible feeling that all was not well. What if Jenny needed him? What if she never received his letters? Her father would not be above keeping them from her. He should have gone back. Years ago he should have gone back. He realized that now, and now he did not have the money.

No matter how tired he might be, Joe always barreled along as though he had a train to catch. Darkness forced him to walk more slowly now, sometimes feeling his way with hands outstretched through the black woods. When he saw flames flickering orange in the clearing ahead, he speeded up again and strode into camp.

Ned sat on a log puffing thoughtfully on his pipe and did not look up as Joe helped himself to a supper of beans, biscuits, and coffee before settling on a stump on the far side of the fire.

Hungry, Joe shoveled a big spoonful of beans into his mouth. He leapt to his feet. His tongue was on fire, the skin scorched off the roof of his mouth, his eyes popped out of his head, but he couldn't swallow without scalding his throat. He grabbed the tin cup of coffee, took a gulp of it and realized, too late, it was hotter than the beans. He danced from one foot to the other, around the fire, but refused to waste a speck of food. Food was too precious up here. He bit off a chunk of biscuit and moved it about with his tongue, trying to sop up the hot coffee and beans.

His partner looked on calmly, puffing on his pipe, as if he were quite accustomed to such performances from Joe. When he was finally able to swallow, Joe took another bite of biscuit. "It's here all right," he said in a parched voice.

At first Ned didn't seem inclined to answer. He took his pipe from his mouth, leaned sideways, dipped his own tin cup into a bucket of cool water, and handed it up to Joe. "Ye-ah?" he dragged out the word, as though reluctant to put aside his own thoughts. "How much ya figure?"

Joe tipped up the cup, drank every drop of water, and wiped his mouth with his shirt sleeve. "Hard to say. I'll know better in the morning."

*\*\**

"Told you it was a good find," said Tall Joe as the two men looked over the day's take late the following afternoon. "Must be close to fifty dollars here. First thing in the morning I'll head into town and stake our claim. You'd best stay here and make sure no one tries to steal it."

"No way they're gonna know it's here 'til you show up in town waving a fistful of gold and looking to stake a claim," Ned pointed out. In his forties now, Ned Turner was beginning to tire of this whole business, this chasing after gold. Not as tall as Joe, he had been until recently a large and muscular man, but he was so thin now his skin hung loosely over his frame and he seemed lost inside his torn shirt and breeches. The hair that stuck out under the brim of his hat was curly and as black as the heavy eyebrows that almost joined above his nose, but his thick beard had gone completely gray. There was a defeated look about Ned, as though he had finally realized that the purpose to which he had dedicated so many years of his life, the goal that had once seemed so essential, no longer held any significance for him.

"It's gotta be done," Tall Joe replied in a matter-of-fact tone. "There's prospectors swarming all over these hills, it's only a matter of time 'til they find someone's been digging here. Can't afford to let someone else get our gold."

"Puh," said Ned, more an expulsion of air than a word, "as if there was enough here to cover the cost of the claim."

"More than enough," Joe insisted. "I've got a feeling about this one, right here." He patted his stomach just under his rib cage. "This is the one'll make us rich."

"Puh!" Ned tossed his arm forward in a gesture of dismissal. "Wonder where I heard that before."

Ned was right. As Joe went about his business in Richfield, small groups of men started gathering on the dusty street, talking amongst themselves, leaning against the sides of buildings, hands stuffed in pockets. The men eyed him without ever quite looking in his direction. Ignoring them, Joe slid into a store to buy a new pick and a good, strong shovel. When he came out, the number of men had increased: thin, shabby men like himself, they watched him with a hopeful, hungry look in their eyes. Joe looked them over and was suddenly grateful he had invested in a good pair of boots, strong lace-up shoes that supported his ankles. None of those poor blokes had decent footwear, a few of them were actually barefoot. Joe figured he could outdistance them easily on the rough trail as he strode off into the woods, the way he had come.

Joe was far from the first to stake a claim on William's Creek since Dutch Bill Dietz first found a dollar to the pan in the gravel; he was not even the first to follow Edward Stout to the area below the canyon where a respectable amount of gold could be found without all the time and expense of digging a shaft. Joe's years of experience and his determination to succeed led him to discover this new claim, overlooked by others, near the mouth of a small creek below the canyon.

About three months ago, May it was, William Cunningham claimed to be making two to three thousand dollars a day on the creek. People back in Victoria might joke about Cunningham's blunt letter:

> Times good, grub high, whiskey bad, money plenty.
> > Yours truly
> > William Cunningham.

But it wasn't long after that the population of Richfield began to grow.

Most of the prospectors who arrived in the spring of '62 had already given up in disgust. If the gold was here at all it was darn hard to find and expensive too, because you had to dig a shaft down to the blue clay beneath the surface. With the cost of food gone up to six dollars a day, they couldn't afford to hang around looking for it. Two weeks was about as long as most of them stayed before heading back to Victoria discouraged, tattered, and hungry. Most of the men Tall Joe and Ned started out with had already left.

The party set out from Victoria around the tenth of June. Joe shook his head now, remembering how easy those first few days of travel were, how confident they all had been, sitting on a steamboat, watching the scenery roll past. The five days from Douglas to Lillooet weren't so bad either, between walking the portages and riding a sternwheeler on the lakes. At Lillooet, knowing prices would be so much higher from there on, they bought all the supplies they could carry on seven horses. They voted to travel over the mountains and take the Brigade Route up the river—Joe shuddered at the memory of that wild ravine. But the land soon flattened out and turned down-right pretty as they passed Loon Lake, Green Lake, and then Axe Lake. If it hadn't been for the hordes of mosqui-toes that attacked every square inch of a man's exposed skin, the sixteen days to William's Lake wouldn't have been half-bad.

At William's Lake they enjoyed their last square meal. Joe's mouth watered thinking of the beef, beans, cabbage, pies, milk, and tea they had gorged themselves on that day, as if it were their last good meal ever. Come to think of it, maybe it was. From William's Lake they headed east, struggling up steep cliffs, plowing through swift-running streams, all the time meeting huge numbers of broken-down miners heading for home.

They lost more than one horse in the river and spent hours pulling the remaining ones through mud up to their bellies in miserable, mosquito-infested swamps. Then came miles of dead and fallen trees bleached white in the sun, lying like so many sticks across the ground. The men had to climb from trunk to trunk and guide the last of their horses over them the best way they could.

When seven of their party turned back Ned was ready to join them, but all those difficulties had the opposite effect on Joe. He became even more determined to reach Wil-liam's Creek and he managed to convince Ned not to give up. Once there, Joe resolved not to leave until he accom-plished one of two things: either starved to death or struck it rich.

For many weeks it looked as if he might accomplish the former. But now, at long last, things were looking up. He had found his gold. This time he would not let it slip through his fingers.

Joe stepped out of the trees and looked down the bank. He was several yards upriver from their claim and could see Ned hunched over, hard at work at the river's edge. Not much of a river really, when you thought about it. Compared to the Fraser or even the Thompson, William's Creek was barely that, barely deserved the name creek. It was only a narrow trickle of water winding its slow way through its own shallow valley. Joe smiled to himself, a trickle of gold that would make him rich.

Ned didn't hear him coming and Joe walked right up behind him before asking, in a loud voice, "Watcha got there?"

Ned jumped to his feet and swung around. He let out his breath when he saw Joe grinning down at him. "You should never do that to an old feller!" he grumbled. "One of these days you'll likely give me a heart attack an' you'll hafta cart me all the way to Victoria to find the nearest hospital."

"If you're planning on having a heart attack, you best wait 'til we get all the gold outta here and can retire to Victoria rich and respectable."

"If I'm gonna be rich and respectable I'll be buyin' myself a piece of land, not wastin' my time havin' a heart attack. Smart thing to do would be for us to buy some land together—British citizens can pick it up for next to nothing nowadays—and get us a farm going. We'd make a fortune selling food to all these miners going by, hoping to get rich from gold."

Joe didn't answer but studied the wooden machine Ned had built while he was away. Joe had never seen a man so talented with his hands as Ned. He had created a slick-looking rocker and was now piling in sand, gravel and water. He rocked it as gently as a mother rocks her baby until all the sand and gravel fell through the grid. Grinning, he picked out the flakes of gold left behind.

"Don't tell me you still got that fool notion of going back to Lancashire to collect your girl? She'll be long since married by now, have ten babies, and not even remember who you are. There's nothing left for either of us back there."

"I need to see for myself."

"Waste of time and money," Ned told him and started to pump the rocker so furiously it cut off all chance of further conversation.

Joe watched his partner, wishing he knew how to explain why he felt such a need to return to England. He and Jenny had known each other since they were young children. Jenny, the parson's daughter, and Joseph, son of the schoolteacher. They had always known they would marry one day. For some reason Joe could not fathom, things had not worked out for them. Maybe it was foolish to go back after all this time, but he needed to find out what happened.

Ned stopped the rocker. "Whew," he breathed, "will you look at that?"

Joe bent his long legs into a crouching position. He

reached down and picked up a thick nugget, as big as the end of his thumb. He rubbed it between his fingertips, grinning.

"Didn't I tell you..."

"One nugget won't make us rich," Ned pointed out, sifting through the grit to pick out several smaller bits of the shiny yellow metal.

A sharp sound, the clink of rocks striking together underfoot, made them both swing around. "Who'er you?" Ned demanded.

The man was small and pathetically thin; his long, sunken face was grey with grime and his stringy hair hung limply over his forehead and down his neck. He had unusually pale blue eyes, too big for his face, they shifted from Joe to Ned and back again.

"Name's Tim. Thought yer might be lookin' to hire some help."

"Where'd you come from?" asked Joe.

"Richfield. Follered yer."

Ned growled under his breath.

"We don't need any help right now, you wasted your time," Joe told him. "You'd better clear out before my partner here gets angry. He's real bad-tempered and you never know what he might do." Both partners remembered the gold rush days in California where there was no law and order and men would kill to take over a rich claim.

Tim did not appear the least bit offended. "Well then, I'll just be movin' on down the crik. Aim to do a little prospectin' on my own."

"See you stay off our claim," Ned warned him.

They kept straggling in after that, swarms of desperate men. Ned worked furiously, ignoring them, or turning to shout at them until they hobbled away over the rocks. Joe felt bad, they had come this far, some limping along barefoot, the least he could do was turn them away politely.

It soon became apparent that they weren't going to get rich. Nothing like William Cunningham. But with steady work they might take out $300 a day for the season. Which meant almost two more months if they were lucky and the bad weather held off.

"Looks like we'll have enough to get that farm started after all," said Ned one evening. He leaned over the fire to stir the beans before settling on a stump with a tired sigh.

That was one thing about Ned, when he thought something was a good idea, he assumed Joe would come around to agreeing with him sooner or later. Joe didn't bother to set him straight.

The nights were beginning to close in on them, the sun set earlier and earlier, and this night, toward the third week in August, there was a definite chill in the air. They sat by the fire, almost too exhausted after a long day's work to wait for the beans to warm up and the bacon to fry.

"It was a good day," Joe said. "I'll bet we took in close to $500."

"Yup. Better'n that poor fool Barker down the creek. Imagine diggin' down more than fifty feet, still hopin' to find gold. Some folks just don't know when to quit!"

"I suppose he's got nothing better to do after jumping

ship and heading all this way. He can't very well head back with nothing to show for his trouble."

The next day, about noon, they were working hard when they were surprised by shouts coming from downstream. They looked up to see Tim making his way across the gravel, waving his arms frantically. "Did ju hear 'bout ol' Billy Barker?" he called.

"Not a word," Ned called back. "What'd he do, have himself a heart attack and tumble into the shaft?"

Tim shook his head but didn't answer. Ned watched impatiently as Tim stumbled over the uneven ground, trying to hurry, filled with the importance of the story he had to tell, savoring his knowing while they could only wonder. When he was close enough, he stopped, shifted from one foot to the other, rubbed a grubby hand over his caved-in face.

"Either start talkin' or get outta here," Ned told him, "we don't plan on standin' around all day starin' at the likes o' you."

Joe had not bothered to stop working and now bent over to scoop a load of gravel into the rocker. It had been a good day so far, they must have taken close to $400 out of the ground since dawn. He didn't want to stop, not for a minute, fearing his luck would run out if he did.

Tim drew a huge breath and spat it out along with the words: "The man's done it, just like he said."

Ned stared at him, speechless. Joe straightened up, clutching the loaded shovel in both hands. The hairs on the back of his neck stood on end, a powerful feeling began to rise up inside him, a feeling of hope, but, at the same time, a strange sort of disappointment. He opened his mouth but found he could not speak. He was barely aware of turning the shovel over and letting the gravel fall into the rocker. He leaned on the shovel, with one end dug into the ground, and studied Tim.

"Done what?" Ned demanded, his voice a tight whisper.

"Only hit just about the richest pay dirt ever seen!"

The silence stretched out, disturbed only by the swooshing of the creek as it slid past the three men.

Tim grinned, just as if he were the one who had struck it rich. "How you boys doin'?"

"Gettin' by," Ned told him.

The silence returned, Tim shifted nervously and glanced from one man to the other. He rubbed his hands together. "Guess I'll be gettin' down there then. Hear there's free whiskey for all who show up. Ol' Billy's havin' himself a cell-ee-bration."

He started to walk away but stopped and turned around. "You boys comin'?"

Ned glanced over at Joe with such an eager, excited look on his face that Joe felt his anger rising at the unfairness of it all. So Billy Barker, a sailor, took a chance and struck it rich. Well, he and Ned might not have hit the big one but they were doing all right. Better than most. "Later," he replied, "I don't want to quit right now, while things are going good."

"Suit yerself," Tim gave a half-wave and turned to stumble away in his thin-soled shoes.

Ned stared at the ground. He looked up at Joe. "If you don't mind…" he began.

"Go!" said Joe. "Doesn't bother me. But any gold I find while you're off celebrating I plan to keep for myself."

"Fair enough. Only…"

"What?"

"Maybe you're due for a break. We've been working every day. Not even stopping Sundays."

"I tell you I'm not quitting. I plan to take every dollar I can out of this place before winter sets in. Then I'm giving up this business forever. It has been far too long already."

"Yer not kiddin'," Ned turned and followed in the direction Tim had gone.

For the rest of that day and all of the next Joe worked the claim. Whatever gold he found, he placed in a separate bucket for himself, alone. Things were looking good, he figured he'd made close to $800 already, working by himself. Ned was a fool, going off, wasting his time.

The next day and the day after that, as he worked, Joe kept looking up, expecting to see him, but Ned didn't return. On the fourth day he began to worry. Ned was not what you might call diplomatic. More than once, when he had said something stupid, getting men all riled up, Joe had had to step in and haul him out of trouble. So, late in the day he made his decision. First thing in the morning he'd go looking for his partner. Funny, they had been partners for so long now they rarely thought about the fact that they were cousins—the only living relative either of them had in the world.

As it turned out, Joe didn't have to go looking for him. Just before dark Ned staggered into camp, sank down onto his back on the dry earth and, without a word, put his hat over his head. He groaned softly.

"What happened to you?" Joe demanded.

"Shhh, don't talk so loud," Ned whispered. "I think I might be dying."

Joe lifted Ned's hat and peered down at his face. Ned covered his eyes with his hands. "My head!" he complained. "It's too bright out there with the sunset an' all."

"Phew!" Joe dropped the hat back over his partner's face, "You smell like a barrel o' whiskey gone sour."

"Feel like one too," Ned moaned.

"Well just keep your fool mouth shut and I'll make us some coffee and biscuits." As Tall Joe gathered wood to start the fire, he wondered if he should tell Ned how much he had earned while his partner was off celebrating someone else's good fortune.

Emma carried a huge platter of food into the room. She held it at shoulder height, which meant the roast duck was just inches away from her face and the tempting aroma floated about her nostrils. Two weeks ago Emma would have sampled the food before leaving the kitchen, would barely have been able to resist stuffing handfuls of it into her pockets for another day. Today she was very proud of herself, she was not even tempted to take the tiniest nibble of the food. Of course, she had not been truly hungry since she came to the Douglas household, not once. What had she ever done to deserve such good fortune?

She would never get used to seeing so much food in one place: salmon, duck, beef, potatoes, pies. How could anyone possibly eat this much day after day? Surely there came a point when you could not cram one more morsel of food down your throat no matter how hard you tried?

She glanced at the men seated round the long wooden table with Governor Douglas at its head. Most of them were old, or at least looked old to Emma. They had round faces with puffy cheeks and chins that never seemed to end but just kept going, one under the other, until they squeezed themselves into the high collars of the men's shirts. The shirts looked wretchedly uncomfortable too, like chokers. The men's necks must get awfully tired of holding their heads up so high, and just look at the way their eyes bulged out—like the round eyes of frogs. So, that was one good thing about being a girl, she did not have to wear a high, stiff collar.

Emma lifted the platter higher and squeezed herself sideways between the backs of chairs and the sideboard. There was not much room because several of the men had their chairs pushed far back from the table in order to accommodate the size of their stomachs. Glancing down from so close, Emma wondered how they ever managed to bend over and pull on their boots. She tried to imagine what it would feel like to walk around never seeing what your own feet were doing.

As she moved along behind them, the men were quiet, respectful, as always in Governor Douglas's home. No fooling around here. The governor expected only the best behavior and always got it. Emma glanced in his direction and away, careful not to gasp aloud. He was a gruff-looking man and right now his dark, piercing eyes were staring right at her; they bored into her and made her want to shrivel into a piece of dust even though she had no idea what she might have done wrong. Emma figured just about everything she did when he was watching would be wrong so she tried her best to stay out of his way. She must not look again, not even a glance, for fear she would drop something, or worse—fall flat on her face.

The silence rose upward from the table; it surrounded her, made her nervous, as though she were an unwelcome intruder or a spy from some enemy camp. She could feel the weight of too many eyes upon her and so kept her head bowed. The silence and the eyes were enough to make her stomach churn. Endless time passed before she reached the middle of the table, squeezed between two chairs, leaned over, and placed the heavy platter on it. As she backed away she happened to glance up. A youngish man on the far side watched her, his blue eyes laughing. When he winked she ducked away and scurried back to the kitchen.

The conversation resumed as soon as she was out of sight. She thought they might be arguing, but it was somewhat difficult to tell for certain. She had never heard anyone argue so quietly before, or so politely. If you didn't hear the words clearly, but just the tone of voice, you would think they were saying nice things to each other. Emma stopped just inside the kitchen, listening, trying to make some sense of it.

"My dear Dr. Helmcken, I should have thought that you of all people would support me on this."

Governor Douglas spoke in a soft voice that did not fool Emma for a second. In less than two weeks she had figured out that a quiet tone did not necessarily mean he was pleased. He was a big man, not overweight but powerfully built, and always held himself very straight, as though he were in the army. He had large hands, a broad face, and a wide mouth that turned down steeply at the corners. His hair did not begin until high over his forehead but it grew long enough to curl around his ears and twist over his shirt collar. Altogether he had an imposing look about him and his most impressive feature was his eyes. They missed nothing, and approved of less. He had a very cold, dismissive way of dealing with people who failed to live up to his expectations, and to Emma his expectations seemed impossibly high. Even his own son-in-law, Dr. Helmcken, was not immune to the governor's criticism.

"You must understand sir. It is nothing against you, yourself, but I happen to agree that a more representative government would be best for the colony."

"I see," said Douglas. His voice sank to such gloomy depths that no one else seemed able to speak at all and the strained silence was broken only by a the clink of knives and forks on china plates. Emma tiptoed away, afraid with every step they would hear the creak of a floorboard or the crackle of her own joints and know she had been eavesdropping.

"He's not so gruff as you might think," said a soft voice.

Emma jumped. Mrs. Douglas looked up from stirring a huge pot on the wood stove, a half-smile on her broad, kind face.

"He is a good man but he will not stand for any foolishness or laziness, not from anyone."

"No," Emma answered quietly and wondered which half of the statement she was saying no to.

"He believes he understands what is right for the colony and does not take kindly to those who interfere."

"No," Emma repeated. She could not imagine interfering with Governor Douglas.

There was a knock at the back door and Emma hurried to answer it. She swung it open and stood gaping in surprise.

The young man on the doorstep smiled at her, an open, white-toothed smile that made his eyes twinkle. He removed his hat to reveal thick, light brown hair that curled over his forehead and behind his ears. "I remember you," he said, "from the day they made all you girls parade down the street like prizewinning horses! You looked angry enough to throttle someone, if you could only figure out who. Can't say I blame you."

"I remember you too," she said. "You were the only one with the good grace to look embarrassed." And you smiled at me, she added to herself.

He nodded. "Yes. I could only imagine how my own sister would feel if she'd had the bad fortune to be one of you."

Emma waited, wondering what *good* fortune had brought him to her door.

"I've brought you the eggs."

She stared stupidly.

"From over at Beckley farm."

"Oh, Yes! Please, bring them on in."

"Edward!" called Mrs. Douglas the moment the young man stepped into the kitchen. "You're just in time for a cup of tea. Come sit down and meet our Emma."

He stayed for close to an hour, chatting and laughing with Emma and Mrs. Douglas. Emma found herself being unusually quiet. She did not understand why, but her voice did not seem to work as well as usual.

When he got up to leave he turned to Emma. "Mind if I come by again?" he asked politely.

"No! Of course not!" she said and tried to fight down a foolish grin that seemed determined to spread across her face.


The several jobs of picking up after the men, washing all the dishes, and scrubbing the kitchen until it shone took hours; but once done, Emma had only to bring in enough firewood for overnight and bank the fire in the wood stove so it would last until morning. Then she was free to do as she pleased.

She could hardly wait to get to her room—her room! Her very own room, that had once belonged to several of the Douglas girls but up until last year when Alice eloped, had been Alice's alone. Little Martha had a small room near her parents and young James also had a room of his own now that most of the children had left home.

Emma's room contained a bed of her own, she did not have to share it with anyone. She had never seen a bed like it before, so big half a dozen people could sleep in it—not a simple bundle of rags in a dirty corner, more than a straw-filled mattress on the floor. It was a mattress set on a wooden frame and covered with blankets so clean she was almost afraid to touch them those first few days. All of this—the food, the house, the bed—seemed outrageous to her. She felt almost guilty having so much for herself. And yet she would not give it up. Not now, not ever.

She closed the door quietly then turned to the room with a quiet thrill. She was alone. As alone as she could ever hope to be; alone to think and plan and dream. One day, when she was rich, she would have a house like this of her very own. She would have at least two girls to work for her and they would carry platters of food to the table. Just like Governor Douglas, she would sit at the head of the table looking very important, talking with her friends, both men and women. The others would all admire and envy her but she would graciously encourage them to talk and laugh and have a wonderful time—oh, and mind they did not pester the serving girls.

Emma put down her candle on the small table near the bed and pulled the folded newspaper out from under her arm. She tossed it onto the bed and then took several steps back to make a flying leap. She was in midair when she remembered Governor Douglas was at home tonight. She could almost see his face pull tight in a grimace when she hit the bed with a crash that could be heard throughout the house. He would turn to his wife and shake his head slightly as if it were all her fault. It wasn't of course. How could Amelia Douglas have known Emma would turn out to be a bed-leaper when she hired her? Emma hadn't even known it herself, having never seen such a bed. But now that she had, leaping up and landing softly in the middle of it seemed like the most wonderful thing a person could do.

She listened. The house was quiet. The world was quiet. Leaning back against the headboard she pulled the *British Colonist* newspaper toward her, opened it up and squinted at the small print in the poor light, doing her best to read the words. It was no use. There were simply too many long words that she could make no sense of; the best she could hope for was a vague understanding of what each article was about.

The owner of the newspaper, that same Amor de Cosmos who had come to look them over on the steamer, wrote mean things about Governor Douglas, she knew that much at least.

There was more news about the gold fields in British Columbia, especially some place called the Cariboo where a month and a half ago a man named Billy Barker had struck it rich. Mrs. Douglas had told her about it.

She put down the newspaper and let her head fall back on the pillow to do some thinking. Her hand went automatically to the ring, still tied around her neck by a piece of Mrs. Barnes' wool. She pulled the loop of wool tight on her neck and began to turn the ring round and round, twisting the two lengths of wool around one another as she often did, unconsciously, when deep in thought.

The tension of the wool at the back of her neck vanished. She looked down. The ring lay loose in her hand, she picked it up and slipped it onto the ring finger of her left hand, surprised at how snugly it fit. She held out her hand, palm down, the fingers slightly outstretched. The pale white oval of the stone sparkled with warm pink lights in the glow of the candle and suddenly she was looking at her mother's hand. Her mother's old and gnarled hand, with knuckles so swollen and painful at the age of thirty that she had been able to squeeze the ring only onto her baby finger.

Her mother's life had been terrible, what with being poor and hungry, with never a decent place to live and a child to care for from the time she was seventeen. Emma saw a chance to make her own life better and she intended to take it. She would let nothing stand in her way. Leaning over, she blew out the candle and curled up in the dark, the fingers of her right hand lightly touching the ring.

Mam would want her to make good use of the ring, Emma was certain of it.

**E**mma left the house just after one o'clock and set out across the bridge. The sky was clear blue but a cold wind whisked across the harbor and over the bridge, forcing her to keep one hand on her hat. With her other hand she held an empty basket and clutched her shawl against her chest in an attempt to keep warm

"Emma!" a voice called from behind. Without looking, she knew it was Edward.

She turned, waved and continued on her way, not wanting any company, not today, not even Edward. There were things she had to do; things that no one else must know about.

She heard the thud of his footsteps, catching up. He touched her shoulder and when she stopped, grinned down at her like a big, friendly sheep dog. She couldn't help but smile up at him. Edward was always so good-natured, and not so bad looking either, in her opinion.

He was a young man of about seventeen with arms and legs that appeared to have grown too fast for his body, so that he often seemed to lose track of where they were and had to consciously force them under control. Emma looked up at masses of curly brown hair which he flicked away now from his round, friendly blue eyes.

It was impossible to dislike Edward. Since the day they met he had stopped by several times a week when his chores on the farm were done or when he had a delivery to make. She was glad enough to have someone close to her own age to talk to, although sometimes she wished he wouldn't come by quite so often. She felt a need to keep distance between them, to pull back from the friendship he offered.

"Got some news for you," he said happily and started walking by her side.

"Yes?"

"Found out where your friend Mary is at, like you asked."

"I didn't ask you to find out, I just said I wondered where she was."

"Far as I can see, it's the same thing."

Emma couldn't help smiling, he was so pleased with himself. "All right then, Edward, where is she?"

"She's working as a housemaid for Mrs. Steeves over on a farm near Constance Cove. None too happy from what I hear."

"I'm not surprised, that woman looked to have all the generosity of a slum rat."

Edward's eyebrows raised in surprise, then he grinned.

"Thank you, Edward. I'll try to visit her on my next half-day off."

She said that, knowing she would not. She would never visit Mary. Edward had called her a friend, but she wasn't really, not like Mrs. Barnes had been, nor Elizabeth Buchanan either. No, Mary was just someone she knew from the ship and it was best she remain that way. If you didn't care about anyone then you couldn't be hurt; no matter what happened, they could not take anything away from you. Emma didn't need friends. She didn't need anyone. Not Mary, not Mrs. Douglas, not Edward. No one.

She walked a little faster, huddled into the wind, thinking her own thoughts. Edward kept pace with her. By the time they reached Wharf Street Emma was anxious to be on her way, she had so far to go. She stopped walking and looked up at him, trying to think of something to say, a way of asking him to leave without hurting his feelings.

"Well, I suppose I'll see you in a day or two, Emma," he said before she could open her mouth. "I'll be off now to visit my mother and the children."

"Goodbye then." She watched him go and wondered why she felt a little hurt that he didn't want to accompany her.

The road to Esquimalt was rough and filled with potholes, but still quite passable. Emma had been told that in the winter, when the rains came, the road would be a river of mud that would sink wagons up to their axles. So she was grateful for having this late October half-day off, possibly her last chance before next spring to get the information she needed.

Next spring. It seemed so far away, but she knew it would be impossible to put her plan into action until April at the earliest.

Around a bend in the road a couple of ragged looking men came strutting toward her. Gonophs, she thought with a quick upsurge of fear. She glanced about, seeking a place to hide, but with thick bushes on both sides of the narrow road there was nowhere to go. For a moment she wished Edward were with her, no one would dare bother her with him at her side. But he wasn't here and she had only seconds to think what to do. Her empty basket would identify her as a servant girl on an errand, the perfect *kinchin lay.*

She had no money. Emma brought the basket merely for show, in order to look as though she had a purpose. The only thing she had of any value was the ring. Quickly, with her left hand hidden behind the basket, she twisted the ring on her finger so it would appear to be nothing more than a plain gold band.

The men were very close now. The younger one was very tall and as thin as a rake, but he walked with a sure and easy step that made Emma think he must be unusually strong. Under a crumpled, wide-brimmed hat, his hair grew long and thick, curling over the collar of his plaid shirt and down past his shoulders. It was the same rich brown as Emma's own hair, but the tall man's full beard had a touch of red in it. Although his clothes were dirty and worn looking, the contented smile on his face made him look unlike any gonoph she had ever seen in Manchester.

The other man was older, although not so old as Governor Douglas. He was shorter than the first man, and not so thin but rather large and muscular. Nevertheless, his body seemed somehow too small for his torn shirt and breeches, as if he were wearing someone else's clothes. His hair was also long, but very curly and black, and his hat perched on top of it like a too-small lid. The thick beard drooping over his chest like a bib was also curly but was completely grey. It was split in two by a huge grin.

Why were they smiling? Must be in anticipation of robbing her, of taking for themselves whatever money she might possess. Emma pulled herself up tall, lifted her chin, tried to look unafraid. She walked briskly, taking long strides in spite of the long cotton skirt that came down to the tops of her boots.

About three feet from her the tall man glanced at her face and stopped as suddenly as if he had crashed into a wall. His smile faded; his face went rigid. His dark eyes widened and he stared down at Emma as though she were some sort of apparition. His mouth fell open, but not a sound came out.

Emma stopped too, undecided whether to turn around and run for her life or scream as loud as she could for help.

The shorter man, having taken several more steps was almost beside Emma when he swung back to his friend in surprise. "What's gotten into you? You look as though you've seen a ghost."

The tall man didn't move and his companion turned to

Emma whose heart was beating hard against her ribs. "Sorry miss, er, uh…" he glanced at the ring on her left hand, "missus? I might say you don't look near old enough to be a missus. Anyhow, I must apologize for my partner here. Been too long since he saw a pretty girl is my guess."

"What's your name?" the tall man asked, his voice not much more than a whisper.

Just then she heard voices ahead, more people coming along the road from the direction of Esquimalt. "Not that it's any business of yours, but it's Emma. And my friends are waiting for me up ahead." Skirting around the strange man as far from him as possible, she ran toward the voices.

"Wait," he called, "where're you from?" But Emma only ran faster.

On her way back to Victoria, Emma was far more cautious. She walked as quickly as she could, afraid as she rounded each bend that she might come face to face with strangers. Her trip had been worthwhile, if discouraging. Everyone she spoke to on the dock told her she was foolish to even think about going to the Cariboo. For one thing the cost was too great, for another the gold mines were a man's world and no place for a woman, let alone a young girl. Not only that but most of the men who went up there, dreaming of untold riches, came back broken and disappointed, without a penny to show for their endeavors. Emma thanked them for their concern and asked about the cost of passage across the strait to British Columbia and beyond, as far as a steamer could take her.

Once safely back in Victoria, she walked up and down the covered sidewalks, studying the stores, deciding which one to approach. It had to be one she had never been in with Mrs. Douglas, she could not afford to be recognized. Finally she noticed a very small wood frame store squeezed between two brick buildings. The sign in the window advertised fine cloth for ladies' dresses as well as jewelry and other accessories.

The proprietor stood behind the counter and looked her up and down as she entered, taking in her decent clothes, not fancy but serviceable enough. The dress had belonged to Alice Douglas, and Mrs. Douglas had altered it to fit Emma. The man's skin was darker than any she had seen before, a rich dark coffee-color; his eyes were large and liquid brown; his hair black but mixed with gray, like pepper and salt. "May I help you?" he asked politely enough but without enthusiasm.

"I hope so," she said. "I have something I want to sell. She twisted the ring from her finger and held it toward him. "I'd like to know what it's worth."

The man accepted the ring, held it up to the light, examined it carefully. "Now, I don't normally purchase goods from customers, you understand," he said, "but this is a mighty fine piece of jewelry. Matter of fact, a man came in just today, looking to spend some of his hard-earned gold. Wants a gift to take home to his sweetheart—as if she'll be sittin' there waitin' for him after all these years. Could be I can locate him before he ships out."

"What do you think he'd pay for it?" Emma reached for

the ring and slipped it back on her finger. She wasn't about to leave it with any stranger.

The man studied her for a moment as if surprised she did not trust him. "Hard to say. Tell you what, why don't you tell me your name and how to find you. If the man turns out to be interested, the three of us can get together and agree on a price. I only ask for twenty per cent. Fair enough, don't you think?"

"Very fair," Emma agreed, thinking quickly. She dared not tell this man she worked for the Douglas family. Governor Douglas would be sure to find out and insist upon knowing why she wanted to sell the ring. She could never tell him about her plans because she was certain he would stop her from setting out for the Cariboo.

The shopkeeper was watching her closely now, his eyes narrowed with the beginnings of suspicion. "I'll come back in a few days," she said and stumbled out of the shop.

Her breathing was ragged and her heart fluttered nervously as she hurried back across the bridge. Too late she realized what a foolish thing she had done, she was too impatient, that was her problem. She should have waited, biding her time until spring, until she was ready to leave. Then, and only then, should she sell her mother's ring and find out about sailings to British Columbia. What a fool she had been! For now, she could only hope Governor Douglas did not hear about her blunder.

Two days later Emma crossed the bridge again, this time on some genuine errands for Mrs. Douglas. She was tempted to avoid the shop where she had inquired about the ring, but kept recalling the look on the man's face when she hesitated for so long to give her name. If she did not return, surely he would take her for a common thief and report her to the authorities. No. The risk of not returning was far greater than that of going back. She would simply tell him she had changed her mind, did not want to sell the ring; at least not just yet.

After bustling about, making her purchases in record time, she ducked into the shop. Two women stood at the counter, talking loudly to one another while the shop-keeper looked on patiently. Dressed in expensive clothing with wide, crinolined skirts, they fingered a bolt of cloth laid out on the counter. Several other bolts lay beneath it.

"No, this one is closer but not quite right. I'm thinking of a deeper shade of blue. What do you think, Isabelle?"

"This most definitely is not you, but either way, your dress will need some lace." She turned to the shopkeeper. "Can you bring us some samples of lace and a darker blue cloth?"

The shopkeeper glanced at Emma and raised his eye-brows as he turned to retrieve more goods from the back room.

Emma waited, watching, looking out the window, making a strong effort not to tap her foot, while the two women attempted to find the exact shade and quality of fabric they wanted. If they did not hurry up she would have to leave. Mrs. Douglas needed her to help prepare for dinner guests.

At last they turned to go, having purchased nothing

other than a short length of lace. "Good day, Mrs. Steeves, Mrs. Morris," said the shopkeeper as he began to re-roll the bolts of fabric. "I hope you'll find something to your liking next time."

They walked toward the door without so much as a thank-you. The first one had the door open when her companion happened to glance over at Emma who had retreated as far into the corner as she could possibly get. Emma instantly recognized the cold, blue eyes that fell upon her, but with effort kept her face blank, hoping Mrs. Steeves would not remember her.

For all her finery, the plump, middle-aged woman had a sour look about her, as if life had failed to live up to even the least of her expectations. A large hat kept her face in deep shadow but failed to hide the hard, thin line of her mouth. The top half of her body stuck out of her huge skirt as though she were being slowly devoured by some enormous fish.

"I remember you," she said in a loud voice. "Aren't you one of those poor wretches who came over on the *Tynemouth?*"

Emma debated her answer. If she said yes, she would be admitting to being a poor wretch, which she did not intend to do. If she said no, she might be accused of lying.

But the woman seemed quite content to answer her own question. "Yes that's right. Aren't you the troublemaker? The one dear Mrs. Robb kindly warned me against?"

Again Emma could not answer. If she did, she would have a few things to say about "Dear Mrs. Robb," not one of them kind. And why would anyone think she was a troublemaker? Mary was more of a troublemaker than Emma had ever dared to be, but she knew Mrs. Robb had never liked her because of her limp.

"I see you haven't managed to find yourself a husband yet, which is to be expected under the circumstances. Let me think, aren't you working for Mrs. Douglas?"

Emma nodded, glancing toward the back room, hoping the shopkeeper had not heard.

"Well," she said, turning to follow her companion to the door, "it's so sad our governor chose to marry that woman. He could have done so much better had he married a well-bred English lady."

"Are you a well-bred English lady?" Emma asked, surprising herself.

The woman stopped. "I beg your pardon?"

"I asked if you are well bred," Emma repeated, feeling herself sinking in further, knowing she should stop, but too angry at this woman who flounced about as if she were better than those around her. As far as Emma was concerned, Mrs. Douglas was a kind, generous person and she would not have her talked about in this way. "You see, I didn't realize that 'well bred' and 'snob' had the same meaning."

"Well, I never!" The woman's jaw dropped, she headed quickly for the door, got halfway through and came to a sudden stop. Emma moved closer and saw the hoop in the woman's skirt pressing against the doorframe on each side. With a grunt and a tug she was through and did not look back as she scuttled down the street.

Emma shut the door and turned around. The shop-

111

keeper nodded at her from behind the counter as he picked up another bolt of fabric. Even though he said nothing, the twinkle in his eyes told Emma he had heard every word.

"Could be I have a buyer for that opal ring of yours," he said, "if you're still thinkin' of sellin' it."

Well, but should she? She wished she had never gotten herself into this. Her first impulse was to run out the door, but that of course would be foolish. He knew where she lived now; he could easily track her down and would certainly have reason to if she bolted. She had no choice but to go through with this and hope word never got back to Governor Douglas.

"Yes, of course I do," she said, and tried to sound very businesslike. "May I ask who the buyer is?"

"Sure can. He's a man staying at the Colonial Hotel. I'll send my boy to fetch him if you can wait a while."

"No, not now, I have to get back." Good. Maybe this would be the end of it. The man would leave town, the matter forgotten.

"All right then, how about your next half-day off. Wednesday, is it?"

She nodded.

"Does two o'clock suit you?"

She nodded again.

**M**rs. Douglas was waiting for her when Emma got back. As she reached out to take the heavy basket from Emma, she happened to look down at her hand. "I never noticed your ring before," she said, "it's pretty."

"Yes," said Emma, suddenly self-conscious. "It was my mother's. I used to wear it around my neck on a piece of wool but the wool broke."

Mrs. Douglas seemed very interested, perhaps she realized that such a ring was not something a poor English girl should have in her possession. "Do you know where your mother got it?"

"Yes, from my father. It once belonged to his grand-mother and he gave it to my mother before they got married."

"Do you remember your father?"

She shook her head. "No, he died before I was even born."

"Oh, I'm sorry," she said, setting the basket down in the kitchen. "Life has not been good to you."

"It's better now," Emma told her, "since I came here." The words slid out of her mouth before she had a chance to think about them but she suddenly realized how true they were. She could not hope for a better employer than Mrs. Douglas and here, in this new world, there was at least some hope for the future.

The days dragged by so slowly it seemed to Emma that Wednesday afternoon might never come. One minute she was optimistic that everything would go smoothly and the next she became frightened that Governor Douglas would find out and make sure she never carried out her plans. He would be disappointed in her, she knew, and that would be bad enough, but to have Mrs. Douglas disappointed in her would be even worse. Mrs. Douglas would think her ungrateful for wanting to run off to British Columbia. So Emma came to fear the approach of the big day.

Tuesday evening, Emma carried a stack of dirty dishes into the kitchen behind Martha who, at eight years of age, helped with many of the chores. Just as Emma put the dishes down, Mrs. Douglas came up to her. "The Governor wants to talk to you in the parlor," she said quietly.

Emma's heart jumped. Had he found out about her attempt to sell the ring? Would he want to know why she needed the money? She knew he would never approve, he was so uncompromising. Just look at the way he treated his own daughter, Alice. She had run off last year, made a foolish marriage which she already regretted but he would not hear of her coming back home. He said her duty was to her husband now, no matter how the man treated her. Imprisoned for life, thought Emma, as she walked on shaking legs toward the parlor, all for one foolish mistake.

"Come in, Emma," he said without the trace of a smile.

"Yes, Sir."

She stood in front of him. He looked into her face and his large, dark eyes were not unkind. "A serious complaint has come to my attention concerning your behavior."

Emma tried to speak but her voice deserted her. She swallowed.

"It seems you were impertinent to one of the ladies of our town?"

Emma nodded, her cheeks burned.

His lips pulled tight, his thick eyebrows lowered. Now he would fire her, she would be out on the street with nowhere to go. Who would help her once Governor Douglas had rejected her? His mouth opened, "I would like to hear your side of the story."

She gaped. Really? Her side?

"You called Mrs. Steeves a snob, as I understand it, may I ask why?"

"I was that angry, Sir."

He waited.

"She thinks she's better than Mrs. Douglas, Sir. She said you would have been better to marry a 'well-bred' English lady. I only asked her if well bred and snob have the same meaning."

"I see." He rubbed his chin, thinking. Then he leaned

forward until his face was very close to hers, his voice was a gruff whisper. "Never tell a soul I said this, but I could not agree with you more." He sat up straighter and in a stern voice added, "See that it never happens again."

Emma almost danced out of the room.


The next afternoon, as soon as her chores were done, she set out in rain so heavy she could scarcely see where she was going. The harbor had vanished in a gray mist and a cold wind drove sharp needles of water against the side of her face as she crossed the bridge.

Outside the shop she stopped to shake rainwater from her shawl and skirt, then, taking a deep breath, she pushed open the door and stepped soggily inside. The shop was cool, gloomy, and empty. She stood uncertainly, deciding what to do. Maybe he had forgotten. Maybe the buyer had already left town. She opened the door and closed it again, a little more loudly than before.

There was a noise from the storeroom and a boy of about eleven emerged. He had short curly black hair, big brown eyes and a serious look on his young face. "You lookin' for my dad?" he asked.

"Yes."

"You the lady with somethin' to sell?"

Her head swung around, looking to see who had come into the shop behind her, but no one had. *Lady?* Never in her life had she been called lady before. Was he making fun of her? Emma squinted at him, studied his face, but she could detect no hint of mockery. "Yes," she said again.

"Then come on back here an' I'll show you the way."

Emma followed him past shelves of many colored fabrics to a set of open wooden stairs. "Up there," he said, "that's my dad's office. Just knock on the door."

Emma's mouth went dry. Was this a setup? Was the ring worth more than she knew, enough to make it worth their while to murder her, throw her body in the harbor, and sell the ring themselves? She studied the boy again, uncertain what to do. Back in Manchester she would never have let herself into a situation such as this.

"Well go on," said the boy. "We don't have the whole day."

He had an honest look about him, she would give him that. Besides, for all they could know, Mrs. Douglas knew exactly where she had gone. Emma trudged up the stairs and knocked on the small door at the top. It immediately swung open. "Ah, just on time," said the shopkeeper.

Emma gasped. Behind him, seated in a wooden armchair in the tiny upstairs office with his long legs stretched out in front of him, was the man who had so frightened her last week on the road to Esquimalt.

Even though he looked quite different today, she recognized him right away. He was faultlessly clean, his hair had been cut short, his beard trimmed neatly, and he wore a new suit of good quality clothes. It was the eyes that she could not forget—those deep, dark eyes that already seemed strangely familiar to her and that stared back at her now with a look of amazed disbelief. He leaped to his feet as the shopkeeper drew her into the room.

"Mr. Bentley, allow me to introduce you to, er,

Miss...?" he turned to Emma. "I don't believe I caught your name."

"This is Emma," said the other man, before she could answer. Mr. Bentley turned to face her. "I remember you from a week ago. We met soon after Ned and I got off the boat." His eyes continued to study her face, as if searching for something, until Emma, acutely uncomfortable, let her gaze fall to the floor: wide, unfinished planks covered in a thick layer of whitish dust.

"I'm glad we met again."

Her head jerked up at the sound of his voice but, with effort, she kept her face expressionless.

"I wanted to ask where you are from, but you ran off too quickly. You look amazingly like a young woman I used to know back in Lancashire County."

"Manchester," Emma told him. "I'm from Manchester."

"I knew it! Everything about you—except that your hair and eyes are a darker brown—is exactly the same. You speak like her too. The resemblance is astonishing! So strong that you have got to be a niece, or a young sister born after I left. You must know her, Jenny Curtis is her name."

Emma felt herself go limp, as if every muscle in her body had suddenly collapsed. She stumbled, unseeing, to a chair and sank into it. She curled forward, folding her arms over her stomach as if in pain.

"What is it?" asked Mr. Bentley, sounding alarmed. He hurried over to crouch in front of her. "You do know her then? When did you see her last? How is she? Tell me, did she ever marry?"

"Jenny Curtis was my mother!" Emma whispered, but her voice caught so completely in her throat that no one heard except herself.

It was then that he noticed the ring. She saw him stare at it. She saw his legs slowly unbend. She heard him speak but his voice was so far above her head it did not seem to belong in this room at all, and her mind did not register the words. "I'll have that ring back now, you had no right to take it from Jenny. I gave it to her, it belonged to my grandmother, and Jenny would never have given it away willingly, no matter what her circumstances, I know her that well at least."

Emma's head was swirling, unable to take everything in. This man, this Mr. Bentley, seemed to be claiming the ring was his. But it was her mother's ring and before that it had belonged to her father. Trembling all over, inside and out, she forced herself to look up at him and was immediately sorry. His face had turned to stone, transformed by anger into something frightening, hideous. Her gaze slid to the floor. "You don't understand..."

"Oh but I do. I understand all too well. You may have the looks of Jenny Curtis but you most certainly do not have her character—why, you're nothing but a common thief. Tell me, how did you take it from her? Steal it when she was asleep?" He paused, "I hope you didn't hurt her?"

"She gave it to me," Emma whispered, desperately trying to sort things out in her mind. How could this horrible man know so much about her parents? He must have known them back in the village where they grew up, he looked to be about the same age. But he could not possibly have been a friend, no friend would use such information in an attempt to steal the ring from her.

All of a sudden she could not imagine ever parting with it, not for any amount of money. This ring was the only thing she had of the mother she loved and the father she had never known. Why hadn't she realized that sooner? She put one hand over the other, covering the ring, sheltering it. This ring, this memory, was more important than any gold.

Now, after all these months of pushing her aside, of avoiding the pain, Emma needed to cry for the loss of her mother. But not here, not now. She pressed her lips tight together, held the tears back.

The man placed a heavy hand on her shoulder, she felt the pressure of his thumb against her collarbone. "Listen, you're very young and therefore I'm willing to be reasonable. If you hand the ring over quietly, I won't go to the authorities."

Emma jerked sideways away from his grip and jumped to her feet. She looked defiantly up into his face. "I will never let you steal my ring."

At this the shopkeeper, whose eyes had been flicking from one to the other, his face frozen in bewilderment, stepped between them. "Look," he said to Bentley, "I can not stand by and let you take the girl's ring because of some story you could have made up for all I know. There's got to be a civilized way to settle this."

"We'll settle it one way or another, Mr. Johnson, if I have to rip the ring from her finger and take it home to Jenny."

"She's dead! Don't you understand?" Emma screamed at him. "Jenny Curtis is dead!" In some small part of her mind, she saw his anger collapse before she swung around and ran from the room almost blinded by her own tears. She could not see the stairs as she hurried down them but clutched the handrail to keep from falling.

She was vaguely aware that the boy stopped what he was doing and stared at her as she burst from the back of the shop; several customers turned to watch as she fumbled with the door handle, flung open the door, and darted outside. Once on the street she knew only that she needed a place to hide, a place to be alone, where she could give in to her grief.

She began walking, forcing back her tears, trying not to be noticed. As she approached the bridge, she looked beneath it to the rows of pilings that rose out of the mud of James Bay. No place to hide there, not even at the ends of the bridge, not a tree or a bush to offer shelter.

On the far side were the Birdcages, that odd collection of buildings in which Mr. Douglas carried on his governing. She did not dare go near there. Nor did she want to go back to the Douglas house and face sympathetic looks or worried questions.

To the park, that's where she would go. Luckily the rain had stopped and a watery sun poked through the clouds. Emma quickened her pace, knowing she would find a secluded spot, a dry hiding place under an arbutus tree in Beacon Hill Park where she could sit and sort out her thoughts.

\*\*\*

Hours later, Emma emerged from the park feeling more weary than she had in many months. She still had not figured out what to do. If this man insisted on calling her a thief, what chance did she have against him? She was a poor girl, brought to the colony out of the generosity of others. She was a child who had no friends. Judging by his appearance, Mr. Bentley was a man with money who could easily take her ring and have her branded as a thief. Unless she surrendered it voluntarily. But she would fling herself into the harbor before she would ever do that.

The hiss of raindrops began to slice through the barren treetops and spatter the earth around her as Emma hurried toward her home, shivering in the cool, damp air, limping worse than she had for weeks. The sky loomed low and angry just above the trees, already closing in to darkness. Coming around the final bend, she looked ahead toward the front of the Douglas home and stopped abruptly on the trail. Instinctively she shrank back into the shadows. Someone, an unusually tall man, was running down the front stairs into the rain.

Her first thought was to run away but she quickly rejected this idea. She was already cold and wet and looking forward to the friendly warmth of the house. Besides, where would she go? Surely he would soon look up and spot her? And she could never outrun him, not with those long legs of his and her with this burdensome limp. Better to confront him within sight of the house than on a lonely trail where he would have the upper hand. Pulling her shawl close about her shoulders, she put her head down against the heavy rain and made a dash for the house.

Joe Bentley stared at the closed door. The girl's footsteps clattered down the stairs as her words repeated themselves in his mind. "Jenny Curtis is dead. Jenny Curtis is dead."

He slumped into the chair she had vacated. All these years he had been hoping, planning for the day he would go back for his Jenny. Even on his blackest days, when he told himself she had married Thomas Brooke, he had not completely given up hope. He would return home, she would see him, they would fall in love all over again, and she would agree to return to British Columbia with him, to start a farm of their own just as they had always planned. He never allowed himself to believe that she might have children now, responsibilities she could not possibly abandon.

On his good days he created an entirely different scenario. Jenny's father had reached Joe's letters before

Jenny ever saw them. He had destroyed them and attempted to convince Jenny that Joseph, the son of a schoolteacher, who had nothing to offer a wife, had forgotten all about her. Her father had tried to convince Jenny to marry Thomas Brooke but Jenny had refused. Instead, she had become the governess to a rich family and even now awaited his return.

Whatever happened, one thing he had never imagined was that Jenny might die before he saw her again. All those years wasted. All this money he now had—for nothing.

"Sir? Mr. Bentley?"

Bentley looked up groggily, as though he were just waking from a deep sleep.

The shopkeeper hovered over him. "Are you all right? You don't look so good. Shall I send my boy for a doctor?"

Bentley forced himself to his feet. "No. I'm fine. Sorry to trouble you, I'll be on my way now."

He stumbled down the stairs and out onto the street where he stood looking back and forth, deciding which way to go. A water cart had stopped in front of a nearby saloon for a refill at a standpipe. He watched without really seeing, took a few steps toward the saloon, then headed off in the opposite direction. Drinking would not solve his problem, neither would returning to the hotel where Ned was making his plans to pre-empt land for a farm on the route to Cariboo.

He took the bridge across the Inner Harbor and soon found himself negotiating the slick mud of the road to Esquimalt. Dark clouds hung overhead but the heavy rain of earlier in the day had stopped. He walked and thought about Jenny, and about how he had wasted their chance at happiness by running off on a foolish scheme to get rich. They would not have had much had he remained in Lancashire and married her but they could have managed somehow. Now it was too late. Jenny was dead. This young girl had her ring.

Who was she anyway? She looked to be about fifteen, which meant she would have been only two years old when he left. He could not remember a child that age in Jenny's family. Perhaps Emma was her sister's child, the sister who had married that parson (what was his name?) and moved to Liverpool. Odd that she looked so much like Jenny.

Bentley began to wonder about the girl. Perhaps she had told the truth. Perhaps, on her deathbed, Jenny had given the ring to a favorite niece. Perhaps she had known the girl was coming to this part of the world and asked her to look out for him, to give him a message if she found him. And now he had frightened her off with his angry words. He had acted more like Ned than himself, the way he lost his temper at the child. If he could only speak with her again he would be more civil.

Suddenly he no longer cared about the ring. If Jenny had given it to the girl, then it was rightfully hers to keep, and he would tell her so. But he needed to know how Jenny had died. He hoped she had not suffered greatly.

Having decided to talk to Emma, he continued on a little farther, giving himself time to clear his mind. He had walked for about fifteen minutes more when he slipped and almost fell in the mud. Ahead was a huge puddle that covered the width of the road. His new boots were coated with mud. The sky above the treetops was growing darker, threatening rain. He turned around.

Bentley walked up the path between two large oak trees to the big, white frame house with shuttered windows. He took the four steps up to a long covered front porch and knocked on the wooden door. After a brief wait the door was opened by a heavy set woman with dark hair and a broad face. Her smile when she greeted him seemed genuine enough, but she took one look at his mud-covered boots and stepped outside rather than invite him in.

"The girl washed the floor before she left at noon," the woman explained. She looked up and offered her hand. "I'm Mrs. Douglas, what can I do for you?"

"Joseph Bentley," he returned the handshake, "it's a pleasure to meet you, Mrs. Douglas. Actually, I came here about the girl, Emma, I am hoping to speak with her."

Mrs. Douglas narrowed her eyes suspiciously while she looked him up and down. "She is very young," she said.

Bentley stared at her. "Yes," he agreed, "she can't be much more than fifteen."

"Thirteen is more like it. Too young for marriage if you ask me. You see, Emma has had a hard life up until now. Her mother died in poverty only this year and Emma still will not talk to a soul about it. Even if she was shipped out here on a brideship, she needs plenty of time to recover before she will be ready to think about marrying."

"Yes," he agreed, surprised to learn Emma was so young. But that explained why he had no memory of her, she had not yet been born when he left England. Still it was odd that Jenny's sister would have died a pauper. Surely, if her parson-husband died and left her penniless, she could have returned to her father's house.

Bentley slowly realized that he had been standing, stone-still while Mrs. Douglas observed him, waiting for some sort of answer. He now saw that she had opened the door and stepped inside. With the door half closed, she turned to speak to him. "So, you will not be bothering Emma Curtis?"

"No," he shook his head, confused. "I only want to speak with her about Jenny."

"I don't know anyone by that name. I must go now before the bread burns in the oven." She disappeared, leaving him standing on the porch, staring stupidly at the closed door. Rain began to thunder upon the narrow roof above the porch but he barely noticed it. He turned and hurried down the stairs. Rain pounded over him, filling the turned-up brim of his hat; it soaked into the jacket of his new suit but still he didn't notice. All he could think about was Emma. Mrs. Douglas had called her Emma Curtis. Who could she be? Not Jenny's niece as her last name would be different. A young sister? That did not seem likely as Jenny's father had been a widower when Joseph left England—unless he had quickly remarried. No, she must be the child of a more distant relative that he had never met or even heard of, in spite of being friends with Jenny Curtis since childhood.

Another explanation began to gnaw at the edges of his mind, but he was not willing even to consider it.

Walking back through the downpour, his head brimming with a confusion of thoughts, he almost missed seeing the girl as she scurried along the trail. She was bent forward, clutching her shawl, her head bent against the rain, her straw bonnet already drooping around her ears.

"Emma," he said softly.

She looked up, gave a little gasp of recognition, and her eyes widened in fear. She started to dart away, heading in the direction of the Douglas house.

"Wait, Emma, please! I promise not to take your ring. I no longer want it, not since I learned of Jenny's death."

Emma stopped about six feet away from him and closer to the house. She squinted back through the rain, a sorry sight, her wet cotton dress hung limply over her thin form.

Only thirteen, he thought, and yet so tall. Small wonder he had thought her to be older. She was much taller than Jenny had been at seventeen when he last saw her. This girl's father must be a very tall man. Again he pushed away a stray thought, one that was too painful to face.

"I loved Jenny Curtis and wanted to marry her, but foolishly I ran off to seek my fortune first, thinking I could offer her a better home. Please tell me, when did she die, and how?"

He stepped toward her but stopped when Emma backed away.

She glared at him. "As if it's any of your business, she died last winter in a nethersken. She was sick and hungry and the room we lived in was filthy. She wore herself out trying to make a life for us."

His heart lurched. A nethersken? Jenny? Then it was true, she died in poverty. "She was your mother?"

Emma frowned, "Of course, I told you that!"

"And your father?"

Her face hardened. "Why should I tell you anything? You were nothing to her, she loved my father and he died."

"He died? Tell me, when did he die?"

At this Emma's face crumpled. "What's it to you?" she managed and turned away.

"What was his name?" he called after her as she ran splashing through the rain toward the house.

Emma ran up the front stairs, pushed through the front door, and took the two flights up to her room at record speed. In a burst of anger she flung the door behind her. Then, gripped by panic, needing to avoid attention, she swung around and caught it just in time. She closed the door gently, without a sound. Then she limped across to the window and stood staring out at the rain.

What did this man want from her? Why did he ask so many questions, trying to dredge up the past? And how dare he say he had loved her mother and planned to marry her? He had some nerve! Emma knew her parents had grown up in a small Lancashire village together and had been friends since childhood. They had always known that one day they would marry. Her mother had never wanted to marry anyone else. If he had not died of typhus, her mother need not have died so young either; they would still live happily together and Emma's father would love Emma too. She knew that.

She turned from the window to slide open a drawer and lift out the old leather case her mother had given her. Opening it, she examined page after page of her mother's small, shaky handwriting. She dropped each one on the bed in disgust. She could not make any sense of it, could recognize no more than her own name and the name of Joseph, her father.

Now, after not wanting to know for so long, she was suddenly consumed by an overwhelming need to find out exactly what message her mother had left for her. But who could read it to her? The only person she trusted was Mrs. Douglas and she was not certain that Mrs. Douglas could read. If she could not, she might suggest taking the papers to Governor Douglas and Emma was not ready for that. What if he disapproved of her mother's last words? No, she was better to bide her time until she found the right person. She picked up all the papers, folded them neatly, replaced them in the leather case, and put the case back into the drawer.

Except for a trip to the kitchen for food, Emma spent the rest of her half-day off in her room. Some of Alice's old books were still on the shelf. She pulled a few of them off, the ones with the biggest print and the most pictures, and took them to the bed where she propped herself up with a book against her stomach and tried to improve her reading.

\*\*\*

Several times in the next three days Emma almost asked Mrs. Douglas if she could read, but changed her mind. When Edward stopped by for tea on Saturday afternoon, her mind kept slipping away from the conversation. She could not stop worrying about what Mr. Bentley might be up to, and was certain she had not seen the last of him.

Emma was bent over, putting wood in the stove Sunday afternoon when Mrs. Douglas answered a knock on the front door. The girl paid little attention to the murmur of voices in the parlor, Mrs. Douglas's visitors did not concern her. As she washed dishes, she tried to figure out how much money she would have by spring if she saved every penny Mrs. Douglas paid her. Not nearly enough to pay her way to the Cariboo, but then she was having some misgivings about her idea anyway. So many men had returned from the Cariboo in the past month, looking as bad as the poorest wretches in Manchester.

Could she hope to succeed where they had failed? Maybe she was better to stay here where she had a job, plenty of food, and a safe place to live. Could that be why her mother left a secure position? Because of some vague promise of riches?

Emma was drying some spoons when one of them flipped from her hands and clattered to the floor. She bent to pick it up. A pair of boots appeared in front of her, above them a skirt and, far above that, the wise face of Mrs. Douglas, looking down. It was odd how different people looked from this angle, all those wrinkles around the neck and chin that didn't show up when you saw them face to face.

Emma stood up. There was a strange expression in her employer's eyes that Emma could not quite define. It was part curious, part anxious, and perhaps a small part hopeful. An unusual and somewhat frightening sensation came over Emma, a tingling all over her body, a feeling that something momentous was about to happen.

"There is someone here to see you," Mrs. Douglas told her and, without a word, Emma followed the older woman into the parlor.

She was not surprised to see who was seated there. He stood up and offered his hand to Emma. When Emma hesitated, Mrs. Douglas said, "Emma, I understand you have met Mr. Joseph Bentley?"

"Yes," Emma whispered and reluctantly shook his hand, wishing she could turn and disappear from the room, wishing he would stop looking at her with those dark brown eyes, as if he could see right through her.

"Before I begin," he said, "I would like to ask when you will turn fourteen?"

More questions. Emma turned to Mrs. Douglas, who nodded encouragement.

"Next May," she said, "as if it's any business of yours."

"Yes," he said, nodding slightly, "I assumed as much."

Emma wanted to ask why he should be assuming anything about her but he continued before she could organize her thoughts.

"I think we should all sit down," he said. "I have a most amazing story to tell."

Emma glanced again toward Mrs. Douglas but the stern look she received told her there was no hope of escape.

She lowered herself stiffly onto the very edge of a chair.

"The village where I grew up near Liverpool was very small," Bentley began. "There was only one parson and one schoolteacher. As son of the teacher I received a very good education—whether I liked it or not—but, because my mother died when I was born and housekeepers were expensive, we never had a great deal of money. There was also the added burden of Ned, an orphaned cousin, ten years older than myself, whom my parents had taken in.

"Reverend Curtis had two daughters and the younger of them, Jenny, and I were the greatest of friends. We always vowed that one day, when we grew up, we would marry.

"Not long after Jenny's sister married a parson and moved to Liverpool, Jenny and I announced our intentions to our fathers. She was seventeen, I nineteen. To our amazement her father flew into a rage. He would have none of it. He refused to allow his daughter to marry the son of a poor schoolteacher. He had high expectations for his favorite daughter. There was an older man in his parish, one who had bundles of money and could offer Jenny a comfortable life. This man had always fancied Jenny and her father insisted she must marry him, for her own good.

"The only thing I could think to do was become rich myself. And by strange coincidence I had just received a letter from my cousin, Ned Turner, who had left home years earlier and found work as carpenter's assistant on a ship out of Liverpool. At the time he wrote the letter he was in California, working on building a sawmill for a man named Sutter. Some of the workers found flakes of gold in the ditch they were digging and Ned was convinced it was the real thing, even though most of the others weren't ready to believe in it.

"He quit his job and, with some of the gold in his pocket, went to San Francisco where he was lucky enough to find a ship just ready to leave for Liverpool. The captain agreed to carry a letter, which I received six months later in August of 1848. He urged me to come out right away, said we would both get rich, that few people knew about the gold yet, that he would most likely already be rich by the time I arrived.

"Anyway, it seemed like providence to me, coming just when I needed money, and my father recently having died of typhus, leaving me just enough to pay my passage. I made up my mind to go. But when I told Jenny my plans, she begged me to take her with me. She had a little money, inherited when her mother died, and could have paid her way and more. But I refused. Don't ask me why—I was young and stubborn, I did not like the idea that my wife would have more money than myself.

"Before I left, Jenny and I exchanged our own private vows. She promised to resist her father and wait for me. I placed my grandmother's ring on her finger and promised to return for her as soon as possible. We would write to one another constantly, we would be apart for only a year, two at the very most, and after that we would be together forever.

"I left in the late summer of 1848. I can still remember her face as we kissed goodbye, tears streamed down her cheeks. She begged me to change my mind, to let her

136

come. But I refused to listen. I had something to prove to the world and I set out to do it. Now, fourteen years later, I have all the money we could ever need. Even though Jenny never wrote to me, not once, I always planned to go back. I was determined to find her and see for myself if it were not too late for us, if she had not married Brooke.

"You can imagine my surprise when I arrived recently in Victoria and saw a young girl who looked so much like Jenny that she simply had to be related in some way. Emma, when I saw you again, above the shop, and noticed Jenny's ring on your finger, I lost my temper. I'm so sorry, I should never have accused you of stealing. I had no right."

All the time he spoke, Emma remained perched on the edge of the chair trying to shut out his words. She did not want to hear them. Her mother would never have lied to her. Why was this man saying these awful things? He told her he no longer wanted the ring, but maybe this was his round about way of getting it from her.

"Do you understand what I'm saying, Emma?" he asked gently.

She stared at the floor, her head spinning.

He was on his feet now, in front of her. "Emma, will you look at me?"

Still she stared at the floor, at the toes of his boots. He crouched down. She studied his bent knees, his breeches pulled tight over them.

"I have good reason to believe you are my daughter," he said softly, just above a whisper.

"No!" She would have jumped to her feet and run from

137

the room but he was too close, she could not get up without colliding with him. She spoke without moving her eyes, still staring at his knees. "My father's dead! He died before I was born! He would never have run off."

"If your mother told you that it was most likely her way of protecting you, knowing you were not likely ever to meet your father."

Now Emma raised her head, just slightly, so that her eyes were level with his. She recoiled from those eyes. There was something deeply disturbing about them, so dark, so intense, they made her want to push him away. In one swift movement she rose from the chair and stepped to the side of it, away from this horrid man who would go to any lengths to steal from her.

"Why are you doing this? I hate you! And you're wrong—my mother was not a parson's daughter—she was an orphan who grew up working for the gentry. Mister, I don't know why my ring is so blessed important to you. It can't be worth much money, but I tell you this: you'll never get it! Not as long as I'm alive!" With that she turned and ran from the room. In the front hall she stopped, looking about, back and forth, knowing she could not stay here. She could barely breathe, she needed space.

As she headed for the front door she heard the man coming behind her, "Please..." he said quietly and she moved a little faster. Once outside, she ran down the stairs and along the straight front sidewalk.

"Emma!" Mrs. Douglas called after her but Emma kept going, splashing over slick mud into a clear, crisp November day.

Before she had gone very far her hip began to ache. It felt as if two bones were rubbing against one another, sending sharp pains down her leg. She was forced to slow down, but even so every step was torture and her limp became more and more pronounced.

She was cold and had no idea where to go. Already she was sorry for running away. Mrs. Douglas would be disappointed in her, she should have stayed and stood up to Mr. Bentley, no matter what lies he tried to tell. But he was so much older and seemed so sure of himself. How could she possibly compete with him? Who would believe her?

Eventually Emma realized she had wandered onto the Beckley Farm and decided this was the best place to be. She would find Edward, tell him what happened. Surely he would understand.

"But I don't understand," said Edward. "Why would he pretend to be your father if he isn't?"

"I told you, it's because he wants my ring!" They sat on the stairs outside the farmhouse. A pale sun shone down through the bare branches of a Garry oak but the air was cold around them and a damp wind began to gust from across the bay.

"Father or no father, you don't have to give your ring away to him."

Ohh, this was too frustrating. Why did he have so much trouble figuring out what she was saying? It was all perfectly clear to her. "He found out the ring belonged to my father and he's pretending to be my father so he can take it back."

"Hmm," said Edward and frowned annoyingly. "But, if your father gave it to your mother and your mother gave it to you, then he has no right to it, father or no father."

"Will you quit saying that! Father or no father, I hate it! Of course he's not my father. No matter what he says. And I can prove it!"

"Oh, how?" Edward looked interested.

"I have some papers—notes my mother left for me, so I would understand the truth about my family."

"I see. Tell me, what do they say?"

"I don't know," Emma admitted under her breath.

"Pardon me?"

"I don't know!" she shouted. "I can't read them."

"In that case let's go find these papers and I'll read them to you."

"You can read?"

"Of course. There was a school here, in the fort, when I grew up. We all learned to read—like it or not."

"You're shivering," said Edward as he walked back beside Emma. Gallantly he took off his jacket and placed it gently around her shoulders.

Emma snuggled into it, it felt warm and comforting, smelling of earth and fresh air and Edward. But her hip still hurt, she could not hide her limp and he asked her about it.

"It's nothing," she said. "Pain is a part of life for the poor children in England. Hundreds are crippled before they reach your age." She looked at his strong, straight limbs and wondered if he realized how lucky he was.

He reached out and took her hand. "I'm glad you came here," he said.

Emma's mouth fell open. She wondered at the burst of joy that shot through her. "Me too," she said, wanting to pull her hand away but unable even to try. She was quite relieved when he let go, it was difficult to keep him at a distance when he held her hand so gently.

They went through the back door and into the kitchen, pausing to listen for voices. When she was certain all was quiet Emma tiptoed up to her room, grabbed the papers, returned, and handed them to Edward. While he glanced through them, Emma made a pot of tea from the large kettle that always sat on the cookstove and carried it to the table. Edward looked up with an odd expression on his face, an expression that held both disbelief and a strange sort of happiness.

"What is it?" she asked, sinking onto a chair. Her heart was beating too fast, thumping away at her ribs.

"First pour yourself some tea. Then, I think I should read to you from the very beginning."

My Dearest Emma:

I am writing this as I lie dying, and pray that you will find someone you trust to read my final words to you. There is something dreadfully important I have wanted to tell you for a very long time, but never was able to work up my courage.

I had always intended to tell you the truth, one day, when you were old enough to understand. I am not certain why I began the lie in the first place, except that I was so angry with your father for leaving me in such an impossible predicament, I almost wished he were dead. At the same time I was ashamed to have a child born out of wedlock. I tried to protect you from all of that, as well as from the knowledge your grandfather did not want either of us. Perhaps it is better to have no family at all than a family that rejects you.

I loved your father from the time we were children together, that much is true. I loved him even more when I was seventeen and we planned to marry. When my father refused to allow the marriage, I was devastated. He wanted me to marry a man twice my age, a wealthy landowner who was one of his parishioners. My father insisted he was thinking only of my happiness, that I would thank him one day, when I was mistress of a grand house and had everything I could ever want. However, I suspect he was doing it more for himself, to improve his own situation. It can be useful to have a rich, influential son-in-law.

Instead of helping me, your father decided to leave me on some crazy scheme to seek his fortune in California. Before he left, the two of us held a marriage ceremony of our own and he gave me his grandmother's ring, the same ring I plan to pass on to you very soon. Please, take good care of it for me.

I was heartbroken when your father left, but soon became angry instead. There was no reason he could not have taken me along, save his stubborn pride. My father continued to pressure me to marry Thomas Brooke and I almost gave in, I was so disappointed in your father. However, to my horror, I discovered a child was on the way. Imagine my panic, my fear, with nowhere to turn for help. If my mother had still been alive, I know she would have protected me but, as it was, I had only my father and he could be a very harsh man.

I considered running away. If there had been one place to run to, one person who might have taken me in, I would have gone. Briefly I considered my sister but decided her husband would reject me, being a man of the church, like our own father. If even there was a chance at finding a job, at building a home for my baby and myself this would have been enough. However, the only possible position for a young lady was that of governess and no family would hire a governess with a child of her own.

In desperation I gathered my courage and went to my father. I told myself that he loved me, whatever happened, and although he would be furious, he would not throw me out on the street.

I was wrong. My father gave me until the next morning to get out of his house.

I left with little money and few possessions. I tried everywhere to find work but with no luck. At last, destitute and half-starved, I turned to the workhouse. Life in there was not worth living: dirty, crowded, with sparse food and no privacy. The people who ran it delighted in their own cruelty. When I began to suspect that my baby, you, would be taken from me as soon as you were born, I ran away. For days, I wandered about, cold, hungry and increasingly desperate.

At last, able to go no farther, I sank down beneath a tree to spend the night. By chance a poor old woman found me in the morning and took me in. She had once done very well spinning cotton in her tiny cottage but recently the mills of Manchester had taken most of her business away. Even so, she had managed to bring in enough to keep from starving until her fingers became so gnarled and clumsy she could barely work. Her eyesight also began to fail. I took over her work.

I stayed with her for over two years and although we had very little, we were content. We grew a few vegetables in the small garden and seldom went hungry. You were born and gave me a reason to live. You also made the woman's last months happy ones. When she died, her son took over the cottage and I was forced to move on.

Emma, that's when you and I moved to Manchester and the cotton mills. The rest of the story you can fill in for yourself. I had no more contact with my father although I know he could have traced us easily enough until I left the old woman's cottage. As to your own father, he too could have found us up until the time we moved, we were not so far from home and the countryside was, by then, sparsely populated. I suspect he never returned from the gold country, perhaps he married over there and forgot me.

For many years I hated Joseph Bentley for the hardships he caused in my life and even more so, in yours. Finally, now as I approach my final days, I find it in my heart to forgive him. I know he would never have left me had he known about you.

I pray that when you hear this message, you will forgive me and your father also. I shall always love you and watch over you,

Your loving mother,
Jenny Curtis

Edward's voice faded away. Emma stared straight ahead. On the other side of the small, square window, naked tree branches swayed in a strong wind, the last of the brown leaves flew sideways through the air. Emma's eyes burned, her throat hurt. She closed her eyes. Could this really be happening? It all seemed so much like a bad dream.

"You're lucky!" said Edward.

She opened her eyes. Her voice refused to work. Nevertheless Edward seemed to guess what she would say.

"To find your father like this and you didn't even think he was alive, you're lucky. My father died when I was only six, he was heading back to England on business when his ship sank off Cape Flattery."

"Oh," she said, "I'm sorry."

"My mother took in laundry, did seamstress work, and anything she could to support us children. Now I'm helping her out by working on the farm, but the pay isn't very much I'm afraid."

"I see." Why was he telling her this? It had no meaning for her, not right now.

"That's why I think you're lucky. You found your father when you thought he was dead—*and* he has lots of money. He can take care of you. So, what do you want to do? Shall we go find him?" Edward started to push himself up from the table.

Emma turned her eyes to him, puzzled. "Why should we? No one needs to take care of me. And why should he suddenly start now after all these years? He never wanted anything to do with me or my mother."

"He didn't know you existed until he found you here," Edward reminded her, sitting down again. "Whatever happened in the past, he deserves the chance to explain himself to you."

"I never want to see him again," she said and, leaving Edward staring after her, walked stiffly toward the door. Mrs. Douglas was standing there, her kind eyes watching Emma with concern. Emma had not heard her come into the room and wondered how much she had heard. She went to her bedroom, sat on the bed, and picked up the leather case, now empty.

Emma was still sitting on the bed hours later, clutching the leather case on her lap and staring at the darkness outside when someone knocked at her door. She didn't answer, hoping whoever it was would go away.

"Emma!" Mrs. Douglas called. "Emma, I'm coming in and bringing you some supper." The door opened. Emma did not turn around. Her head ached, she was exhausted, all she wanted was to be left alone. The rich aroma of Mrs.

Douglas's thick chicken stew floated toward her, invaded her nostrils, made her mouth water. Emma tried to resist. She was not hungry.

Oh, but she was! She glanced sideways at the tray Mrs. Douglas placed on the bed. A big bowl of stew, some freshly buttered bread, a tall glass of milk, and an apple.

"Go ahead, eat. It doesn't mean you have to talk to me." Mrs. Douglas settled on the opposite side of the bed, at the far end, facing in the opposite direction.

Emma took one taste of the stew, small one, just to be polite; she took another because it tasted so good. She gobbled down the whole bowl of stew and wiped it clean with the bread. Mrs. Douglas said nothing, merely sat patiently, cradling a candle in a holder between her hands.

"I don't need a father," said Emma quietly.

"Maybe not, but it seems like you have one anyhow."

Emma didn't answer.

"What do you plan to do with him?"

Do with him? Why did she have to do anything with him? Why couldn't he just go away, leave her alone? "Nothing," she said.

"Did you notice his eyes?" Mrs. Douglas asked. "They're the very same as yours. So dark and they look right into a person."

"I don't like his eyes," said Emma. "They're scary."

Mrs. Douglas said nothing. The silence lengthened.

"Do I have scary eyes?"

"No. And neither does your father. You have interesting eyes."

"Don't call him that. He isn't my father."

Mrs. Douglas sat very still. She didn't try to lecture, she didn't attempt to influence Emma. She merely sat quietly, letting Emma know that she was ready to listen.

"How can he be my father when he was never there as I grew up?" She paused, pressed her lips together, and then let loose a torrent of words. "My mother told me he was dead and he may as well have been. Mam did everything she could for me. Do you have any idea what it's like for a woman in England to raise a child alone? No one is there to help her—she can die of starvation on the streets and her baby too for all anyone cares—driving by in their fancy carriages! He left her to that; he had no right!"

"He didn't know."

"He should have known!" Emma could hear her voice rising, and tried to control it. Why did everyone take his side? He deserted them when he was needed, and now, with her mother in an early grave, Emma was expected to forgive him? Accept him as the father she always wanted? Carry on as if her mother had never suffered, never so much as existed?

She leaped to her feet, swung around to look at Mrs. Douglas, a dark, solid silhouette with the candle flickering in front of her. Emma clenched her fists at her sides, could barely stand still, barely speak without shouting. She swallowed, even now aware that Governor Douglas might hear. Her voice when it emerged was a fierce whisper: "Why didn't he come back? He said he'd return for her in two years. Why didn't he come back and find us? He was having too much fun, that's why. He's a thoughtless, selfish, cruel man."

Mrs. Douglas sat quietly. Finally she turned her head slightly. She moved the candle just enough so Emma could see her face, deeply shadowed in the soft light, and she could see Emma's.

"After twenty-nine years of living with him, moving wherever the Company sent him and bearing his children, my mother went with my father to Montreal. Before a year had passed he deserted her to marry a white woman. After that he wanted nothing to do with any of us. My mother went creeping back up north to the land and people she knew best and lived for many more years. She died only this year."

"Oh," said Emma, sinking onto the bed. Suddenly she felt bad, not for herself but for Mrs. Douglas. What was it her mother said? *Perhaps it is better to have no family at all than a family that rejects you.*

And here sat this kind woman who carried her own troubles hidden deep inside while concerning herself with everyone else's problems.

"I'm sorry," Emma said quietly. "I didn't know."

"There's no reason you should," Mrs. Douglas told her. They sat facing in opposite directions in a room dimly lit by one flickering candle. "I only told you because you are so alone. You travelled far from your home believing you had no family in the whole world. Now you find you have a father. Seems to me you should give him a chance."

Give him a chance, Emma thought. To do what? It was too late for her mother and, as for herself, she didn't need him. She didn't need anyone.

"He told me he wrote to your mother many times. He

sent her money for passage to California, but she never answered. He thought she had married someone else and forgotten him.

"She promised she wouldn't."

"She also promised she would write to him. How could he know what had happened? Seems to me your grandfather is the one to blame, if you need to blame someone. He must have received those letters, he could have written to your father and let him know the truth. Seems like he should have been sorry for what he did by that time."

"Yes." Emma pressed her fingertips hard against her forehead. There was a terrible pressure pushing outward, filling her brain, making it impossible to think clearly. From being alone in the world she now had a father who came back from the dead and an evil grandfather who had caused all her problems in the first place.

She didn't understand any of this, either of these two men. If you love someone, don't you do everything you can to see that they are happy? If you love someone, you don't put her out of your house when she needs you the most; you don't run off and leave her when she begs not to be left alone. "I'm not ready for this."

"I understand," Mrs. Douglas said. Only then did Emma realize she had spoken out loud. Mrs. Douglas got up from the bed and walked around it to place the candle on the small dressing table near the window. She laid a gentle hand on Emma's shoulder. "I will leave you alone to think about everything."

She was aware of the sun before anything else, the brightness of the room. She opened her eyes, amazed that she had slept so well and for so long. Usually she was up before dawn, building up the fire in the wood stove, preparing breakfast for the family.

Emma could hear distant voices, including a man's. Governor Douglas? Shouldn't he be out of the house by this hour? Why hadn't someone called her? She had a job to do. Or wait, was today Sunday? No, Sunday was yesterday. She sat up in bed and swung her legs to the floor. Everything came back to her in a rush, as if she had been slammed across the chest with something solid, like a brick.

The last thing she remembered was Mrs. Douglas leaving the room, giving her time to think. Emma glanced down: she was still wearing her dress from the day before. She looked at the dressing table: the candle, or what was left of it, a little puddle of wax, lay in its holder, a tiny black wick curling out of it. She must have laid her head on the pillow, fallen asleep, slept right through the night, and not thought at all, not for a second. How could that be? Well, she certainly didn't intend to think about anything right now, she had work to do.

The face of Mr. Bentley, the man who was her father, flashed into her mind; the eyes so sad and lonely, she almost wanted to reach out to him. Or were those her own eyes? She tried to push the image away, forget about it, but it would not go. She tried to summon up the anger she felt yesterday, but it had deserted her. Something had happened while she slept so soundly. Her own mind had betrayed her. But not for long.

Emma jumped out of bed and attempted to straighten her dress. No, it was much too wrinkled; she could not go downstairs looking like this. Quickly she changed clothes. She had so many clothes now, clothes left here by Alice when she had eloped. It seemed she didn't want them any more. The dresses were all far too short of course, and a little loose fitting, but Mrs. Douglas had shown her how to fix them up—add a little fabric to the hemline, take a few tucks here and there.

When she was ready, with hair brushed and neatly pulled back from her face, Emma hurried downstairs. She burst into the kitchen.

"I'm sorry I slept so late. Why didn't you wake me?"

Mrs. Douglas added a pinch of salt to a large pot on the stove and picked up her wooden spoon. At the table, Martha was placing a wrapped loaf of bread into a large basket. "We're going on a picnic!" she said.

Emma shivered. A picnic, in November? She turned to Mrs. Douglas.

"Have you forgotten? Today is the Prince of Wales' twenty-first birthday and the governor declared a holiday. He's just left with young James for the park. Hurry and help us so we don't miss the parade."

No, going to a parade was out of the question. She could use the time to gather her own thoughts together. "I think I'll just stay here, if you don't mind, where it's warm. I can scrub all the floors while there's no one here to get in my way."

But Mrs. Douglas only shook her head, as she ladled thick, hot soup into a large clay pot. "Today is a holiday, no one works today. Besides, we're bringing plenty of hot food, aren't we Martha?"

Martha nodded and gave a little skip. "I don't have to go to school!" she grinned.

"We're meeting Alice and the others there. We'll all dress warmly, I have some things for you to wear—and at least it isn't raining."

Emma groaned softly. Her life, it seemed, was not in her own control.


In spite of herself Emma got caught up in the excitement as Mayor Harris went charging past, leading the race on the track around Beacon Hill, his horse looked like a small pony underneath him and it wheezed pitifully under his weight.

"That poor horse!" Emma said to Edward who had mysteriously appeared at her side.

"I don't know how such an overburdened beast can run so fast," he said. "Thomas Harris weighs at least 300 pounds." He laughed, "Did you hear what happened at the first council meeting last summer?"

"No," Emma watched as a much thinner, much younger man with long legs, a thick mop of brown hair and wide sideburns that met underneath his chin came storming up, almost on the heels of the mayor's horse. She recognized him as the commander of the gunboat that had brought the girls from Esquimalt. Commander Lascelles urged his horse on, slowly gaining on the mayor. Emma expected the mayor's horse to collapse and die of exhaustion at any moment.

"His chair gave out underneath him the minute he sat down. Nothing was left but a pile of kindling."

Emma laughed, "Really? He must have been embarrassed."

"No, he probably just made a joke and demanded a heftier chair."

A third rider broke away from the pack where he had been trapped behind other horses. He barreled forward screaming loud enough to scare all the horses into headlong flight. He was a small man with thick gray hair and a full beard.

"Look at him, he's catching up," said Emma. "He's so small and light, I bet he'll win."

"That's John Howard—he owns the Royal Oak Inn, you know, on the harbor at Esquimalt."

Emma nodded and tried to remember what it looked like. They watched as Howard quickly gained on the other two. A roar rose up from the crowd.

"Those three are great friends," Edward told her, "seems it's always one of them that wins every horse race."

Somehow, at the last minute, with Mayor Harris leaning over its neck and bellowing for it to go faster, his horse put on a final burst of speed and bolted over the finish line in first place.

The crowd cheered, some slapped others on their backs, some laughed, others looked grim. Soon they began breaking into small groups and wandering off in various directions. Edward looked down at Emma. "I'm meeting my family for lunch, would you like to join us?"

"Oh, thank you, but I can't. I'm expected to be with the Douglas family."

Emma watched him lumber off in his amiable way and smiled to herself. He was one person who accepted her as she really was. He had yet to give her a word of unwanted advice and she was grateful to him for that. Happily, she turned away to search for the Douglas family.

There were so many in that family, what with daughters, husbands, children and grandchildren all milling about that Emma didn't notice him at first. When she did it was too late to turn around and disappear.

He and another man were deep in conversation with Governor Douglas. Emma turned her head slightly, tried to watch without seeming to be interested at all.

The third man was large and muscular but not so tall as the other two. He wore an expensive suit of gentleman's clothing, including a long jacket, buttoned vest, high leather boots and a hat with a narrow brim and rounded top. The short hair that showed beneath his hat was very curly and black, but his neatly trimmed beard was completely grey. Not until a wide grin split his beard in two did Emma recognize him as the same man who had accompanied Joe Bentley that first day, on the Esquimalt Road. His partner. What were they talking about? She strained to hear.

"Emma!" Mrs. Douglas called, "I can use your help."

Emma looked toward her employer and saw that she was surrounded by a sea of people, big and small, all demanding to be fed. She hurried over to help.


Later, she found herself sitting next to Mr. Bentley on a blanket spread out over the damp ground. She felt the need to speak to him. Suddenly there were hundreds of questions she wanted answered. But she couldn't think how to begin. She felt awkward and self-conscious. What was the etiquette for speaking to a father one didn't know? The longer she went without saying anything, the more impossible it became to open her mouth. She sensed he felt the same way.

"My partner, Ned, and I are looking into pre-empting some land," he said almost casually.

"Oh?"

"Yes. Governor Douglas gave us some advice. He says

there's good land up near 'The Lakes' on the Thompson River. It's too late in the year now, but Ned and I will go up and take a look around come spring."

"I thought you were going back to England."

"No. There's nothing for me over there now. Everything I care about is here."

"Oh."

"Besides we didn't make enough money to retire for the rest of our lives like bloomin' gen'lemen."

Emma smiled but said nothing.

"Enough to start a farm though." He paused. "Something your mother always dreamed of doing."

Emma made a move to get up, to make a run for it. For what? She had nowhere to go. "Yes," she said, "she loved the countryside."

"Please hear me out," he said and something in his voice, something that hinted of desperation made her want to listen.

As he talked she watched his eyes. Yes, they were like hers, just as Mrs. Douglas had said. Perhaps that's why she found them so disturbing. She looked down at her hands, clasped so tightly on her lap that all her knuckles were white as bones. The pure oval of the ring stood out, so familiar that for a moment she thought she was looking at her mother's hands.

"I realize now that I made a huge, unforgivable mistake," he said. "If there were any way to make up for it—but of course there isn't. It's simply too late. Because of me, Jenny suffered horribly…" his voice choked, he seemed unable to go on.

Emma waited, still looking at the ring. She glanced at him, his eyes met hers and she saw the suffering there. She turned away.

"Tell me, do you think I would have left her had I known about you?"

Emma watched the crowds of people milling about, all of this seemed so unreal to her. A lump in her throat made it impossible to speak. If he had not been so obstinate, if he had not refused to let her mother come with him, how different their lives would have been.

"You think I should have listened to her, have let her come with me in the first place."

Emma nodded. How did he know exactly what she was thinking?

"Of course, you're right."

She glanced at him sideways.

"I have no excuse except that I was young and stubborn and foolish. I couldn't resist the chance of an adventure and the chance to make our lives better, Jenny's and mine. We all do things we regret in our lifetimes. You may be too young to realize that yet."

After a short pause, he added: "Who knows? Your grandfather may even regret what he did by now, provided he's still alive."

She found her voice, or at least a part of it. "I regret trying to sell my mother's ring." If she had not done that, she would not be dealing with this situation right now. She would never have known her father was alive. She would be free of this complication in her life.

Before he turned away she saw the pain cloud his dark

eyes, as if he realized exactly what she was thinking. Something twisted inside of her. Is that really what she wanted? Not to know? If he walked out of her life right now, would that make her happy? *Perhaps it is better to have no family at all than a family that rejects you.*

"I don't need to be taken care of," she said.

"No. I'm sure you don't."

"I can take care of myself."

"I'm sure you can."

"I came this far on my own didn't I?"

"Yes."

"And I have a job?"

"Yes."

Now what, she thought. He seemed so agreeable. Would he walk away and leave her alone now, not want anything more to do with her? With a shock that made her gasp, sit up a little straighter, she realized that she hoped not. Having a father might not be such a bad thing after all. Especially if he was going to be around for a while. But perhaps it was already too late, she had let him know he was not wanted, not needed. Would he slink away and never bother to contact her again? She saw him shift on the picnic blanket, thought he was about to get up. No, please don't go, she thought, but knew she could never say a word out loud.

"How would you feel about helping to build a brand new farm?"

Relief made her reckless, giddy, "Don't know," she said, "I've never done it before."

"Well that makes two of us." He glanced over at Ned

who was dipping a large chunk of bread into his bowl of soup. He bit into the bread and a line of yellow liquid dribbled down into his beard. Bentley chuckled. "Three," he added.

Emma laughed. "Don't you think one of us should have at least some idea of what we're doing?" She was scarcely able to believe this conversation. Was she really agreeing to go off into some wilderness to create a farm with a father she didn't know?

"I'm sure it wouldn't hurt," he admitted with a grin.

Emma looked up, across the crowd. What she saw made her question the decision she had just made. Or had she really made a decision at all? Maybe it was simply talk, simply dreaming out loud. There was a third possible future for her, one that did not involve either her father or the Douglas family. Was this other future something she wanted? She couldn't know for sure, not yet, but she did know she was not ready to throw the possibility away.

"I have an idea," she said, turning back to Bentley, "that is, if you can afford a hired hand. Someone who knows what he's doing. Of course, this person would need to be well paid."

Bentley looked startled. "Well, I suppose we'll need someone," he said vaguely. He looked from her to the young man ambling toward them and then back to Emma again.

She met her father's puzzled eyes, smiled and then turned to look up at Edward. He stopped in front of them, grinning down, happy to see the two of them together.

"Mr. Bentley," Emma said, "I'd like you to meet my

friend Edward Macdonald, who just happens to be an expert on farming. And Edward, allow me to introduce Mr. Joseph Bentley, my—er—my father."

Bentley rose to his feet. Standing several inches taller than Edward, he looked down on him with an odd sort of anger in his eyes, as if Edward had done something to hurt him. Edward didn't appear to notice, he extended his hand to shake, "Mr. Bentley, Sir, I'm very pleased to meet you. I hope you realize what a wonderful daughter you have here."

Bentley hesitated. It almost seemed as if he would refuse to shake Edward's hand. Emma scrambled to her feet and pushed herself between them. She stared into Bentley's eyes, trying to understand what had gone wrong. Her father took one long look at her and his eyes widened, as if he had just suddenly recognized something he had seen before and did not care to see again.

"You're so much like your mother," he muttered before reaching around her to shake Edward's hand. "Pleased to meet you too, young man. Let's none of us repeat the mistakes of the past."

"No, Sir," said Edward, glancing toward Emma with a puzzled frown.

Emma only shook her head, she would try to explain later, if she could. Fathers were complicated creatures, that much she realized by now.

"If you're interested, I may have a job for you come spring."

Edward looked surprised. "Could be," he said, "what sort of job?"

"Helping my daughter here," he paused and smiled slightly, "I like the sound of that, helping *my daughter*, my partner, and myself carve a farm out of the wilderness."

"There's nothing I would like better, Sir."

Emma looked from one to the other, then sank down to the blanket. Everything had happened so quickly. Had she really committed herself to a certain future, filled with people who might very well become important to her? Well no, not quite, she was only thirteen. If it turned out she didn't like farming, or Bentley, or Edward, there was plenty of time to change her mind.

She touched her ring and smiled to herself, remembering the young girl who had sat listening while two men discussed the far-off colony of British Columbia. She had been certain the land would glitter gold wherever the sun touched it. All of that seemed so long ago now, a childish dream. And yet, if all went well, she would be in British Columbia come spring. She watched her father and Edward happily discussing plans, and stood up to join them.

*Actual people from BC's colorful history who appear or are mentioned, however briefly, in this novel:*

**Billy Barker** was born in England. He joined the Royal Navy when quite young but was in his forties in 1861 when he deserted his ship to head for the Cariboo. He dug a shaft below Richfield and the canyon where he thought a deep buried channel of William's Creek would be. Although many made fun of him, they stopped laughing when Barker struck rich pay dirt 80 feet down on the bedrock. While his mine kept producing, Barker spent money lavishly on his new, young wife, on celebrating, and on helping other miners. When he ran out of money there was no one to help him. He died in Victoria in 1894.

**Amor de Cosmos** started life as William, or Bill Smith. Originally from Nova Scotia, Smith moved to San Francisco during the California gold rush of 1849 and from there to Victoria where he started the first newspaper, *The British Colonist.* He decided the name Bill Smith was too common and so chose Amor de Cosmos, which means, "lover of the universe." However, there was no love lost between de Cosmos and Governor Douglas. De Cosmos was premier of British Columbia from 1872 to 1874.

**Elizabeth Buchanan** was one of the young women on the ship *Tynemouth;* she died shortly before reaching the Falkland Islands and was buried at Port Stanley, where the ship stopped for fuel and repairs.

**Miss Angela Burdett-Coutts** was an English-woman who inherited a fortune from her grand-father when she was not yet twenty. She spent most of her life and a great deal of her money trying to help the poor. Among other things she built homes where girls could escape prostitution, and improved housing for factory workers. As a member of the Columbia Emigration Society, she sent 40 destitute girls on the *Tynemouth* to Victoria. Earlier she had sent two archdeacons and a bishop to the young colony. She was good friends with Charles Dickens and was well aware of the huge problems in English society.

Note: The other twenty young women were part of the "London Female Middle-Class Emigration Society," a feminist group formed to send educated women to Victoria; women who were looking for adventure and a self-supporting career. These women either paid their own way or borrowed money from the society.

**John 'Cariboo' Cameron** was born near Glen-garry, Ontario and took part in the California and Fraser River gold rushes. Returning to Ontario, he married Sophia Groves and together they came to William's Creek in the spring of 1862. Cameron dug his shaft a half mile farther down the creek than Billy Barker and he too struck it rich. But by September, when miners began building cabins in the area, Sophia was very ill. When she died, Cameron went through great difficulty to take her body by sled to Bella Coola, from there to Victoria and later home to Ontario. The town that sprung up around Cariboo Cameron's claim became known as Cameronton.

**William Cunningham** was one of the early prospectors who struck it rich on William's Creek; his company took out $270,000 in gold in 1862-63. He did not have long to enjoy his money as he died in Soda Creek, June 21, 1864 of "mountain fever" or typhoid.

**Dutch Bill Dietz** is credited with being the first to discover gold in the gravel of William's Creek. It was February of 1861 and he had to thaw the gravel in the stream before panning. William's Creek is named after him.

**Alice Douglas**, daughter of Amelia and James Douglas. She eloped to Port Townsend, Washington with her father's private secretary Charles Good when she was only seventeen. Upon their return her father insisted they repeat the ceremony in a Victoria church. She grew to hate her husband and later took her children and ran away to England to escape him. But Good brought her back and her father and the bishop forced her to stay with him.

**Amelia Douglas,** daughter of Suzanne, a Cree Indian woman, and William Connolly, chief trader of the Hudson's Bay Company (HBC) for Fort St. James. Amelia had a reputation for being firm with her children but always fair and kind. She married James Douglas when she was sixteen, the marriage was formalized by the church in 1837. She gave birth to thirteen children, many of whom died young. Only four survived her.

**James Douglas** was born in Demerara, British Guiana, in 1803. His mother Martha Ritchie was the daughter of a "free colored woman" in Barbados; his father John Douglas from Glasgow, Scotland, managed a sugar plantation in Demerara.

From the time he was nine, James was educated in Scotland and came to North America when he was sixteen to work in the fur trade. He was sent to New Caledonia in 1825 where he worked for William Connolly at Fort St. James. Much later he became Chief Factor of the HBC at Victoria. For a time he held two jobs: Governor of Vancouver Island and Chief Factor of the HBC; from 1858 to 1864 he was governor of the two separate colonies of Vancouver Island and British Columbia.

**Thomas Harris,** originally from England, later from San Francisco. Harris opened the first butcher shop in Victoria in 1858. In 1862 he was elected as Victoria's first mayor. It has been said that he was more than adequate to fill the mayor's chair.

**John Helmcken** came to Fort Victoria as a doctor to the small colony. He married Cecelia Douglas in 1852 and they lived next door to the Douglases. Helmcken House is preserved as a museum beside the Royal British Columbia Museum which is the site of the Douglas family home.

**John Thomas Howard,** also from England by way of California, where he earned enough money to open the Royal Oak Inn at Esquimalt. He was a sportsman and raised horses.

**Horace Douglas Lascelles** joined the Royal Navy when he was just thirteen; was commander of the gunboat *Forward*, based at Esquimalt, from 1862-1865.

Harris, Howard and Lascelles were good friends as well as great rivals on the race track.

**Mary Moody,** wife of Colonel Richard Moody of the Royal Engineers. Her husband created New Westminster to be the capitol of British Columbia, after deciding that the first selected site at Derby, near Fort Langley, would be too difficult to defend if attacked by the Americans. Two girls from the *Tynemouth* were sent to help Mrs. Moody with her five children. One of them was returned for being "too young, too small, and incapable of sewing." She was replaced by an older girl.

**Prince of Wales,** eldest son of Queen Victoria and Prince Albert. Prince Albert Edward was born on

November 9, 1841. He became King Edward VII in 1901 after the death of his mother.

**Mrs. James Robb** traveled on the *Tynemouth* with her husband and three children, none of whom were confined below decks. She was charged with teaching "all the arts of womanhood" to the girls and to protect them from "lascivious attentions of the crew." The mannerisms and pattern of speech afforded to her in this story are purely fictional.

**Reverend William Scott** traveled with his wife, Helen, and their two children, also not kept below decks. They were on their way to the Sandwich Islands (Hawaii). He was the second chaperon for the young women in third class.

**Edward (Ned) Stout** was wounded in an Indian attack in the Fraser Canyon on his first attempt to reach the gold fields. When he finally arrived at William's Creek he decided to prospect the area below the canyon where no one else believed gold could exist. In May of 1862 he dug deep into the gravel at the mouth of a small creek and found bright, jagged gold, a rich find. It was after this that Billy Barker and John Cameron decided to dig farther down William's Creek. Stout died two years after his discovery, having never quite recovered from his earlier wounds.

# GLOSSARY

*Terms used in Victorian England:*

*BEARER-UP:* bully who robs men decoyed by a woman accomplice

*BOBBY:* policeman; named for Robert Peel who organized the first police force in London; also known as Peelers

*CHOKER:* clergy; or the high, stiff collars worn by clergy

*COSTERMONGERS:* people who sold fruit or other food on the streets, usually from carts or wheelbarrows; established costermongers had a defined territory and did not take kindly to intruders

*GONOPH:* minor thief or third rate pickpocket

*KINCHIN LAY:* robbery of a child; especially one who is obviously carrying money or other valuables

*MOUCHER:* rural vagrant

*NAVVY:* an unskilled laborer who works on canals, railways, roads

*NETHERS:* rent, paid by the poor crowded into filthy lodging houses

*NETHERSKEN:* low lodging house; filthy, overcrowded without heat, water or sanitary facilities

*SKIPPER:* one who moves about the country, sleeping in hedges and outhouses

*TOFFKEN:* house with well-to-do occupants

# *TYNEMOUTH* PASSENGER LIST

Partial list of the young women
aboard the brideship *Tynemouth:*

Emily B. Abington
Sarah Baylis
Elizabeth Buchanan
Mary L.L. Chase
Mary Cooper
Francis Curtis
Isabel Julia Curtis
Jane Eliza
Mary E. Evans
Julia Louisa Hurst
Mary MacDonald
Augusta Jane Morris
Emily Anne Morris

Dayle grew up near the waterfront in Victoria, BC where she and her friends liked to play on the beach. They explored the shore, built forts and rafts, and paddled logs "canoes." Sometimes Dayle liked to imagine that she lived in the early days, before the city grew up on the land above the cliffs.

When alone she loved to read, especially animal, adventure and mystery books. She didn't write stories in those days but made up exciting adventures in her mind. She has such fond memories of those special preteen years that she now enjoys writing for young people.

Dayle and her husband live on Salt Spring Island, BC and have two grown-up children. She enjoys hiking, biking, sailing and exploring her beautiful province, both its past and its present. Her books range from historical novels and outdoor adventures to mystery stories and, occasionally, science fiction.